THE RONNIE GENE

THE RONNIE GENE

JON MILLS

FIVE STAR

A part of Gale, Cengage Learning

GALE
CENGAGE Learning

Detroit • New York • San Francisco • New Haven, Conn • Waterville, Maine • London

GALE
CENGAGE Learning

LIBRARY OF CONGRESS CATALOGING-IN-PUBLICATION DATA

Mills, Jon, 1947–
    The Ronnie gene / Jon Mills. — 1st ed.
        p. cm.
    ISBN-13: 978-1-4328-2516-4 (hardcover)
    ISBN-10: 1-4328-2516-X (hardcover)
    1. Private investigators—Fiction. 2. Murder—Investigation—
Fiction. 3. Fraud—Investigation—Fiction. I. Title.
PS3613.I568R66 2011
813'.6—dc23   2011031290

First Edition. First Printing: November 2011.
Published in 2011 in conjunction with Tekno Books and Ed Gorman.

To my wife, Susan, and our three daughters,
Kimberly, Jessica and Samantha

ACKNOWLEDGMENTS

As this book progressed, I counted on friends to read it and be unsparing with their criticism. "It doesn't help to tell me what you liked," I told them, "I need to know everything you don't like." The following people took that assignment seriously, bless them, and when my bruised ego recovers I will be sure to thank them for their thoughtful comments: Carol Blann, Sandy Brown, Aaron Cohen, Lynn Cohen, Steve Cohen, Sharon Fiffer, Amy Gary, Barbara Gately, Margo Kavanaugh, John Kennedy, Faye Knowles, Joel Leland, Daryl Monfils, Doug Muirhead, Emily Muirhead, Barbara Myers, Joel Ostrow, Len Rubin, Marsha Sullivan, Karen Thomson, Charlene Vickery and Chris Wheeler.

Richard Sugar and Steve Felsenthal and everyone else at the law firm of Sugar & Felsenthal LLP: thanks for your consistent friendship and support.

Five Star, and especially editors Alice Duncan and Laura Patchkofsky: thanks for making it so easy.

My agent, Joan Brandt, introduced herself with a detailed, insightful edit of my manuscript, and gently and gracefully led me the rest of the way through this process. Joan, I can't thank you enough. My testimonial to your skill and perseverance in getting *The Ronnie Gene* published is the fact that I am writing this sentence.

My friend Daryl Monfils is prominent in the promotional game business, a subject we discussed over too much rich food and expensive wine. He told me what happens in the story is plausible. He also explained why it doesn't happen in a respectable company such as his. If you glossed over the small print disclaiming any intentional similarity between characters in the story and actual persons, or if you suspect I didn't really mean it: Daryl was not in any way, even remotely, the model for Stanley.

Three decades ago, when my wonderful wife Susan vowed to love (and she did), honor (and she did), and obey (who was kidding whom?), she surely knew marriage teemed with other vows unstated and implicit, but I don't think she ever bargained for *edit*. Nonetheless, she painstakingly line-edited every draft I gave her (a number way in excess of umpteen), caught mistakes and inconsistencies, and argued and cajoled on behalf of stylistic changes I confess were, for the most part, significant improvements. Whatever she did in a past life to deserve this was her bad and my good fortune.

★ ★ ★ ★ ★

TUESDAY

★ ★ ★ ★ ★

PROLOGUE

There's an obvious reason not to point a loaded gun: it might go off.

The intruders accosted Pete Tilden at gunpoint as he was unlocking the door to his Lincoln Park townhouse. They ushered him to a couch in the living room and began their effort at persuasion.

Pete knew they had no intention of killing him, so it never crossed his mind that he might actually be shot, much less that the bullet that would kill him would, quite literally, cross his mind.

Pete's mistake was to get up and pour himself a scotch. That agitated the intruder with the gun. It wasn't aimed at Pete, just in his general direction. But the intruder's hand was shaking and, as fate would have it, the gun was pointing at Pete's head when the intruder's finger inadvertently squeezed the trigger. The bullet burst from the barrel and flew ten feet until it smacked into Pete's forehead. It lost too much momentum punching its way in to get out, and spent the rest of its energy ricocheting off the inside of Pete's skull, churning tunnels through his brain until it came to rest in his pituitary.

Pete dropped his drink. It splashed over the white Chinese carpet. For a moment he looked surprised, as if he was about to say, *Now look what I've done.* But nothing came out of his mouth until his legs buckled and he dropped to his knees and fell

11

forward on the carpet. What came out of his mouth then stained the carpet red.

The shooter looked at Pete's body, then at the gun, and said, "Damn!"

"That's all you can say?" the other asked. " 'Damn'?"

The shooter shrugged. "It was an accident."

"So what do we do now?"

"We find where he put it."

"How we going to do that? He's dead!"

"Shut up!" the shooter snapped. "We got to think."

They thought.

Done thinking, they ransacked the desk and file cabinets in Pete's den and stuffed the papers into a small green duffel bag.

Then they tore the townhouse apart.

On their way out they walked past a photograph of four young men in graduation gowns. One was the spitting image of Pete, only about forty years younger, with hair down to his shoulders rather than combed straight back and no hole in the middle of his forehead. It was mounted in a wood frame with FRIENDS burned into the top and WISCONSIN DELLS burned into the bottom.

The shooter aimed at the photograph and fired, blasting Pete's head out of the picture, and said, "That's better."

"What is wrong with you?" the other muttered, grabbing the photograph and shoving it in the duffel bag as they closed the front door.

There's another reason not to point a loaded gun: if it goes off, the repercussions are unpredictable. Because bullets that end lives begin investigations. And while a bullet can only go where it's pointed, an investigation can veer off in any direction.

★ ★ ★ ★ ★

Friday

★ ★ ★ ★ ★

CHAPTER 1

In the months since JAMOS & MOSIT, INC., PRIVATE INVESTIGATORS had been stenciled on the frosted glass window of the office door, Stanley Jamos and Dave Mosit had been engaged in precisely zero private investigations.

Stanley had every confidence that over time, he would double that number.

The office was a testament to their success. Jamos & Mosit, Inc., Private Investigators, occupied one room in a building where the rent was low and the amenities nonexistent. The furniture was contemporary eviction, pieces too cumbersome and valueless for the predecessor tenants to bother with when they split without notice, several months' rent in arrears. The landlord couldn't get a scavenger to haul them away without charge, so he left them there and called the room a furnished office.

Stanley picked the swivel-back chair behind the small desk, leaving Dave the red leather high-back. The third chair, a heavy wooden butt-breaker next to the radiator, Stanley sarcastically called the client seat. It had yet to be used. The office was otherwise nonfunctional, undecorated and uninviting. No telephones. No file cabinets. No computers. No carpets. No pictures on the walls.

Vertical streaks of bird droppings, darkened by grime piped from the kitchen of the diner next door, gave the lone window the look of prison bars. The view outside was a singularly depressing panorama of the diner's dumpster, the rear of a five-story brick building across the alley, and the elevated train tracks. Every ten minutes or so a train swept by, shuttling people who, unlike Stanley and Dave, had somewhere to go.

Stanley wore a jacket over a sweatshirt, loose-fitting corduroys and running shoes. The fact that he had no clients to impress gave him the freedom to wear clothes that didn't tax his manipulative abilities.

Dave, by contrast, wore a blue blazer, white shirt with a button-down collar, club tie, black slacks and brown loafers with tassels. He looked prepared for an important appointment. But Dave had no expectations, would have forgotten a meeting had one been scheduled and would have been perplexed by a visitor had one appeared. His wardrobe reflected the deference his wife, Cindy, gave to the neurologist's admonition to avoid changes in Dave's patterns. She dressed him in the same clothes he wore back when he could dress himself to go to work. Except for the tan slacks. Those she'd given away and substituted black, which made his occasional incontinence less conspicuous.

Dave also wore a tan fedora with a green feather in the hatband. It had been peculiarly out of character the first time he wore it some four years before. Stanley had teased Dave about it until his strange unresponsiveness and his obstinate refusal to remove it, even if custom or courtesy dictated otherwise, got him concerned. When Stanley finally got up the courage to broach the topic with Cindy, she alluded to other recent idiosyncrasies.

A year later Dave was diagnosed with Alzheimer's.

A year after that, Stanley, Dave and Pete were out of a job.

The day began like every other.

Cindy dropped Dave off at the diner, said good morning to Stanley and goodbye to Dave, and left.

Stanley never asked her where she went.

Stanley and Dave ate breakfast in silence, staring at their newspapers. Stanley read the *Chicago Tribune*. Dave preferred the *Chicago Sun-Times*.

After breakfast Stanley brought both papers back to the office and read them front to back to kill the time that passed with glacial speed.

At noon they broke for lunch back at the diner, presenting Stanley's daily quandary. Should he sit across from Dave in silence? Or should he invent something to talk about? The former was as awkward as the latter was frustrating, because Stanley would have to remind Dave every few minutes what they'd been discussing. Today they ate in silence until Tracy, the diner's owner, joined them, which she often did when the diner was otherwise empty, which it usually was. She groused about how bad business was. Stanley let her ramble. He never once told her, *I can tell you a thing or two about how bad business can be.*

As Stanley paid the bill, Tracy casually asked, "So what are you up to this afternoon?"

Stanley shrugged. "Not much."

Tracy glanced around the empty diner and frowned. "Ain't it the truth."

Stanley had no reason to think the afternoon would be different from any other.

He would perform his one job, which was getting through the next four hours.

He might read a book. He might field a call from his attorney concerning some aspect of the Jamos Company bankruptcy. He might nap or stare out the window watching for signs of life in the neighborhood, daydreaming that he was young and healthy again and that Jamos Company was still in business. At five o'clock, Jamos & Mosit, Inc., Private Investigators, would call it a day. Stanley would lock the door and walk Dave to the parking lot, where Cindy would pick up Dave. Then he'd drive to the Uptown apartment he rented after the Jamos Company bankruptcy forced him to sell his Water Tower Place condominium.

When they returned from lunch Stanley was suddenly overcome with drooping eyelids, a side effect of the new meds his doctor had recently prescribed. In less than a minute he was dozing on his swivel-back chair, head back, mouth agape, feet propped up on his desk. His nap lasted under five minutes.

Dave poked him.

"Huh?" Stanley muttered, stirred from sleep. He stretched and rubbed his eyes.

Dave pointed out the window.

Stanley turned to see what Dave was looking at. A third-story window of the brick building across the alley was wide open. A man with bushy white hair, wearing a waist-length leather jacket, was standing on the fire escape. A second man, darker hair but in a similar jacket, was climbing out the window, holding the window frame in one hand and a cigarette in the other. White hair leaned over the fire escape, spat and turned up the collar of his jacket against the gusting March wind.

Stanley's immediate reaction was, *Cops. Or hoodlums. One or the other.* Then he panicked, *They're spying on me!* He squeezed his eyes shut and ordered himself, *Calm down. It's just the meds.* He swung his legs off the desk. Doing his best to sound chipper, as if forced gaiety was an antidote, he said, "Well, pal, I don't know about you but I could use a snack." He opened the bottom desk drawer and took out a box of whole wheat crackers and an aerosol can of cheese spread too toxic to bacteria to require refrigeration. He asked Dave, "You want any?"

"Where are we?" Dave asked.

"At the office, Dave. Jamos and Mosit."

"Jamos and Mosit," Dave mused. When Dave thought about something, he looked six rather than sixty, a bewildered little kid with his hands folded patiently in his lap, a motionlessness for which Stanley was exceedingly jealous. "Is that us?"

"That would be us, yes."

Dave gave this information serious consideration. "We're not at Jamos Company?"

Stanley sighed. "No, Dave. This is where we work now. Just you and me." He held a cracker smeared with gelatinous yellow chemicals toward Dave and asked, "Sure you don't want one?"

Dave's brow furrowed but he was otherwise the picture of calm. Dave had always been a worrier but never excitable, characteristics the Alzheimer's hadn't yet decided to change. "Why aren't we at Jamos Company?"

"Jamos Company went out of business, Dave. Been that way for two years now." He withdrew the offer and popped the cracker in his mouth.

Stanley's cell phone rang, a tinny digital rendition of "Surfin' USA." He glanced at the caller ID. A Chicago area code, but a number he didn't recognize. Probably a wrong number, sales pitch or other irritation. He swung his chair around so that he was looking out the window. The men on the fire escape were gone, and the window they'd opened was shut. "Hello?" he answered.

"Mr. Jamos, please? Stanley Jamos?"

"Speaking." At least the speaker's tone lacked the pumped-up enthusiasm of a stock broker on a cold call.

"Detective Chris Birkholz. Police. Eighteenth District."

"How can I help you?"

"Are you at . . ." Stanley heard the sounds of the telephone clattering on a desk and ruffling papers. Then Birkholz picked up the telephone and recited an address.

"That's right," Stanley said.

"Please stay there. We'll be there in fifteen."

"Okay. But can you tell me what this is about?"

"We'd rather discuss that in person."

The line disconnected.

CHAPTER 2

Through the frosted glass Stanley saw the distorted images of two human shapes, one rapping insistently. He got off his chair and opened the door.

A pallid, late-thirties, stocky, beer-bellied, balding man in a dark blue polyester suit barged in past Stanley. His bushy mustache gave his face an amiability his cold, narrow eyes belied. "Birkholz," he said. Thumb pointing over his shoulder he added, "My partner, Detective Hustad."

Hustad was a head taller than Birkholz, gaunt and dark, with sad, compassionate eyes in an otherwise expressionless face. He wore a camelhair coat over a black wool three-piece and Italian shoes. Stanley knew clothes. The package was expensive, not exactly affordable on a cop's salary. That meant Hustad came from money. Or maybe he had a wealthy wife. Or maybe he was on the take.

Hustad attempted a smile and extended his hand.

"Please come in," Stanley said, stepping aside to let Hustad pass.

Birkholz and Hustad canvassed the office. Whatever impression they formed of Jamos & Mosit, Inc., Private Investigators, they were careful not to telegraph.

"I'm Stanley Jamos," Stanley said. "And this is my partner, Dave Mosit."

Hustad nodded to Dave. Dave smiled back.

Hustad's eyes flicked up to the fedora on Dave's head. "Nice

21

hat," he said. Dave's lips parted slightly. A small bubble of foamy drool tried to escape but was sucked back in.

Birkholz yanked the client seat away from the radiator, eased himself onto it and swung his left leg over his right. Pulling a cigarette from behind his ear he asked, "Mind if I smoke?"

"We don't have an ashtray," Stanley said. "Since smoking was banned."

Ignoring the rebuke, Birkholz struck a match on his shoe and lit up.

Stanley slid the garbage can over to Birkholz and opened the window a few inches. Birkholz tossed the match at the garbage can, took a deep drag, and sat back with a contented smile, looking as if he planned to stay a while.

"We don't have any more chairs," Stanley apologized to Hustad. He pushed his swivel-back to the side of the desk and said, "Please. Take mine."

Hustad dismissed the offer with a wave of his hand and said, "I'll stand, thanks." He pulled a notepad from his jacket and a pen from his shirt pocket and busied himself flipping through the pages.

Birkholz reached into his jacket and extracted two cards. He placed one on Stanley's desk, and extended the second to Dave.

Stanley picked up the card and read it as he sat. Printed below Birkholz's name was a single word. HOMICIDE.

"We understand you're familiar with a man by the name of Peter Tilden," Hustad said.

Stanley's shaking hand made the card flutter. He placed it face up on the desk, staring at it, too dazed to speak.

"Mr. Jamos?" Hustad said.

Stanley looked up at Hustad. His voice hoarse, he asked, "Pete's been murdered?"

Birkholz jerked forward. "Did we say that? What makes you think he's dead? How do you know we're not here because Mr.

Tilden murdered someone? Or do you know something we don't?"

"Pete murder someone?" Stanley said, aghast. His left hand began to shake harder. He grabbed the arm of his chair and squeezed to relieve the tremors. "He wouldn't do that."

Birkholz started to respond but Hustad cut him off. "I'm afraid you were right," he said gently to Stanley. "Mr. Tilden's dead."

Stanley sagged into his chair. He heard himself ask, "How?" as if the word was spoken by someone else.

Birkholz raised his hand, thumb up, fingers curled, index finger pointing at Stanley's face. "Took one at close range. Don't have the medical examiner's report yet, but appears he's been dead a couple of days. Either of you own a gun?"

Stanley shook his head. The motion felt wobbly.

"Mr. Tilden's maid found the body this morning," Hustad said. "She goes there every Friday. Lets herself in. Look, we realize this comes as a shock, but we need to ask you some questions." Hustad turned to acknowledge Dave. "You too, Mr. Mosit."

Dave blinked uncomprehendingly.

"You okay, Mr. Mosit?"

Dave turned to Stanley. "What's happening?" he asked.

Stanley said, "Pete's been murdered, Dave."

"Murdered?"

"Murdered," Stanley repeated.

Dave looked perplexed. "He would have had insurance."

Hustad jotted *insurance* in his notebook. "I'm afraid I don't understand, Mr. Mosit."

Dave looked up at Hustad. The fedora was starting to slip off his head, and a thin stream of saliva was trickling from the corner of his mouth. "Pete would have had insurance," he repeated.

Birkholz squinted at Dave. "What's your point, Mr. Mosit?"

Stanley waved his hand to get Birkholz's attention. "Sometimes Dave gets confused."

"Must be contagious," Birkholz said. "Sure got me confused." He turned back to say something to Dave but Dave's expression had gone blank.

"Well, as long as the subject's been raised," Hustad said to Stanley, "you know if Mr. Tilden had any life insurance? Enough to kill him for?"

Stanley removed his bifocals and rubbed his eyes. "Look," he said, "give me a minute."

"Sure," Birkholz said. He stifled a yawn and casually stretched. "Take your time. Don't let the fact that every second counts in a murder investigation interfere with anything." He held up his wristwatch, as if Stanley could read it from where he sat.

"Life insurance?" Hustad persisted.

Stanley put his steady right hand over his twitching left and did his best to compose himself. "Well, when he was at Jamos Company . . ."

"Jamos Company?" Hustad interrupted, flipping to a new page and scribbling the words.

"The three of us, Pete and Dave and I, used to work together. At Jamos Company. Until a couple of years ago."

"Jamos Company," Birkholz repeated. "That make you the big cheese?"

"My father started it. Anyway, all the employees had group life insurance as part of . . ."

"What happened a couple of years ago?" Birkholz interrupted. His eyes swept the room and the corners of his mouth edged up in a sardonic smile. "Sell out for big bucks?"

Stanley felt his cheeks flush. "We went bankrupt."

"No shit." Birkholz smirked at Stanley. "I sort of guessed."

"This group life insurance," Hustad prodded. "You know how much he had?"

Stanley shook his head. "It wasn't a lot."

"Any other life insurance you know about?"

"No. But he had no family, so I doubt he would have needed much."

"So how long did you know Mr. Tilden?"

"We met in college. Wisconsin."

Hustad turned to Dave. "How about you, Mr. Mosit?"

"Dave and I both met Pete in college," Stanley interjected.

"He have any enemies you know of?"

Stanley shook his head. "I never heard anyone say a bad word about him."

"He ever mention feeling threatened?"

"No."

"What about his house? He keep anything valuable there?"

Stanley's left hand was shaking harder. Neither squeezing the chair's arm nor clamping it with his right hand was easing the tremors. He rose, went to the overcoat hung on a peg by the door and removed an orange prescription bottle. He twisted off the cap, popped a pill into his mouth and returned to his chair. His left arm felt like a fish out of water, flopping uncontrollably. He sat and crossed his arms and massaged the fluttering muscles. When he looked up he saw the detectives' attention focused on his arm. Birkholz's gaze slowly climbed up to Stanley's eyes, and locked there.

"Nervous, Mr. Jamos?"

Stanley always dreaded this moment. It meant he hadn't been able to hide it, that his hand and arm had betrayed him once again. No matter how politely it was posed, the question always came through to him as, *What kind of circus freak are you?*

"Parkinson's," he said.

25

"Parkinson's," Birkholz repeated, nodding slowly, assimilating the information. He jabbed a thumb in Dave's direction, his arched eyebrows asking, *What's his problem?*

"Alzheimer's," Stanley said, stress reducing his voice to a hoarse whisper.

"Mm-hmm." Birkholz nodded again. He looked up at Hustad. When he looked back at Stanley, his mouth didn't smile but his eyes crinkled with cold amusement. He took another drag on his cigarette and spat out, "Detectives," in a tone that communicated, *Give me a break.*

Stanley glared at Birkholz. The tension between them hovered like a lingering flatulence until Hustad, sounding apologetic, said, "Valuables? I was asking what he might have had in his house."

"Nothing valuable enough to kill for. Not by Lincoln Park standards, anyway," Stanley said.

"The place was pretty torn up. Drawers and cabinets open, stuff tossed all over the place. Looks like he came home in the middle of a robbery."

"Or it was made to look that way," Birkholz said.

"Problem is," Hustad continued, "there's a couple of loose ends. Leaving the flat screen TVs and audio equipment behind makes it look like they had to leave in a hurry. But none of it was unplugged. See what I mean? If they broke in to take that stuff, the first thing they'd do is disconnect it. Which means maybe they weren't after stuff they could unload on the street."

"Which also means maybe the burglars weren't your average criminals," Birkholz said. "You have any idea what they might have been looking for?"

Stanley shrugged. "Sorry."

"Let's get back to Jamos Company," Hustad said. He opened his notepad. Pen poised to write, he asked, "Anyone there Mr. Tilden didn't get along with?"

Stanley shook his head. "Everyone looked up to him."

Hustad flipped a page. "So after Jamos Company went bankrupt, you and Mr. Mosit formed this agency?"

"That's right," Stanley said. *Before we lost our health insurance,* he added mentally.

"Some reason you didn't invite Mr. Tilden along for the ride?" Birkholz asked. "Like maybe he was the reason Jamos Company went under?"

"I did," Stanley said. "And he wasn't."

"Then who was?" Birkholz asked. "You?" He jabbed his cigarette in Dave's direction. "Einstein?"

Hustad held up his hand. "What my partner wants to know is the circumstances under which your company went out of business. In case there's a connection to the murder."

"There isn't," Stanley said levelly, fighting to control his anger. Anger made his arm flap like a kite in a downdraft.

"Let us be the judge of that."

"It's not that complicated. We overextended our credit. That led to cash flow problems. We couldn't get out from under."

Hustad paused his note-taking and looked up. "Look, I'm no lawyer, but I thought that's what bankruptcy's for. To help companies with cash flow problems get out from under, as you say."

"Yeah. That's what we thought, too."

"So what happened?"

"What does this have to do with Pete's murder?"

Birkholz jerked forward, glaring at Stanley. "Just answer the question, Mr. Jamos."

"It may or it may not have anything to do with the murder," Hustad said. "Too early to tell at this stage. But it's our job to find out. Okay?"

Stanley shrugged and spread his hands. "There's not much to it. We thought Chapter Eleven would be a slam dunk. I talked to all our clients before we filed and explained the problem. They said they understood and would work with us and wanted us to stay in business." He half closed his eyes, reliving the trauma of what came next.

"Go on," Hustad prodded.

"Then one day the termination notices started pouring in. By a week later we'd lost every single one of our contracts."

After Hustad completed his notes he asked, "You know what happened?"

"I sure do," Stanley said bitterly. "One of our competitors started floating rumors that we'd been stealing from our clients. We never found out who."

"Stealing," Hustad repeated, scribbling. "How was Mr. Tilden when this was going on? Did he act any differently?"

"I'll say," Stanley said. "I'd never seen him so angry. If he ever figured out who started the rumors, you'd be arresting him for murder."

"What about the creditors?" Birkholz asked.

"What about them?"

"They can't have liked getting stiffed. Any of them have a beef with Mr. Tilden?"

"What? You're thinking one of them might have . . . ? That's ridiculous," Stanley said. "And besides, they've all been paid. All except the bank."

"How? I thought you were bankrupt?"

"Dave and Pete and I made up the difference. Even the debts we hadn't guaranteed."

"Well, then," Birkholz said. "What about the bank?"

"The company's assets are being auctioned in May," Stanley said. "There's more than enough to pay that off."

"If you say so," Birkholz said. He uncrossed and recrossed his legs. "Who's Ed Lind?"

Stanley's brow creased as he thought. "Sorry. Name doesn't

ring a bell."

"Then can you explain this?" He pulled a sheet of paper from his jacket and placed it on the desk.

Stanley turned it around and read the block letters on a message pad. CALL ED LIND / JAMOS.

"We found it under Mr. Tilden's telephone," Hustad added.

Stanley spread his hands. "I'm afraid I can't help you."

"You know why Mr. Tilden had a flight booked to the Bahamas for yesterday?" Birkholz asked.

"He did?" Stanley said, surprised. "He didn't mention it to me."

"Well, now that you know, got any idea why he'd be going there?"

"Because it's March in Chicago?"

"First he goes bankrupt," Birkholz said. "Then he takes a Caribbean vacation. How do you explain that?"

"He didn't go bankrupt. The company did. And he obviously had enough left over after paying his share of the company debt." *Unlike Dave and me, who are up shit creek,* Stanley added mentally.

"That make you jealous, Mr. Jamos?"

Stanley took a deep breath. "Are you accusing me of killing Pete because he had more money than me?"

"You said it," Birkholz said icily. "I didn't."

Hustad coughed loudly. He emphatically snapped his notepad shut and capped his pen and returned it to his shirt pocket. "I think we're done," he said.

Birkholz ground out his cigarette against the sole of his shoe. "I got one more question. Who's Nick Fitzgerald?"

"Pete, Nick, Dave and I all went to Wisconsin together. Frat brothers. He owns a bar. You need his address or phone number?"

Hustad patted the pocket with the notepad. "Thanks. Got it.

He's next on our list."

"You know," Birkholz began as he slipped on his overcoat, staring down Stanley as he spoke, "people think they can get away with murder. But they can't." He looked at Dave, who appeared to be asleep. "Einstein remembers anything, give me a call," he said, and slapping Stanley on the shoulder added, "and you be sure to let me know what's shaking. Okay?" He laughed. A sadistic, one-syllable laugh.

Hustad let Birkholz leave first. Hand on the doorknob, he turned back to Stanley, rolled his eyes and shrugged.

It was all the apology Stanley was going to get.

Stanley shrugged back. It was all the *Forget it* he was going to give.

CHAPTER 3

It took Stanley less than ten minutes to drive from his office to Nick Fitzgerald's bar. It took over twenty more to find a parking space within walking distance. Five years ago Stanley could have parked in front of Nick's any time of day or night. Then the condominiums and boutiques sprung up, and with them more foreign cars than the street could accommodate.

The neighborhood's gentrification made Nick seem to take pride in his own building's dilapidation. The trendier the street became, the less Nick bothered with maintenance. Standing under the neon *Nick's Bar* sign in the dusk, Stanley observed that its anchoring bolts were coming loose and the facade was in desperate need of tuckpointing.

Inside, Nick was growing uneasy about his two customers.

The woman, Petra, he knew well. She was one of the coterie of women who steered their clients to Nick's, where the dim lighting made the rear booths convenient to deliver their merchandise. Her companion was the real cause of Nick's concern.

He had seemed innocuous enough at first, talking nervously about his accounting practice while Petra feigned interest. The second scotch dissipated his awkwardness, liberating a personality prone to loud, disparaging comments about the ambiance of the bar and occasional vulgarities. He was now on the third and had become bellicose, dropping ethnic slurs as casually as if they were section headings in the Internal Revenue Code.

Nick was bracing for trouble when Stanley walked in.

The man and woman shifted their attention to Stanley as he struggled to unbutton and remove his overcoat. The accountant rolled his eyes contemptuously, judging Stanley's fumbling efforts to be the toll paid for years of substance abuse, and steeled himself against the anticipated plea for spare change. The woman reflexively started to throw Stanley a fetching smile but stopped when she saw the way his left hand shook. It gave her the creeps. She crossed her legs, not to lure but to cover the worst of her varicose veins, and pushed her glass toward the accountant.

"Be a dear and buy me another," she purred, struggling to stifle a yawn.

"Another cosmo!" the accountant barked at Nick, forcing his voice up in volume and down in octave to mark his territory and make clear to the newcomer his claim to the woman.

"Coming right up," Nick said indifferently. He watched Stanley cross the room, reflected in the mirror behind the bar. The crack, which ran pretty much the length of the mirror, made it appear as if Stanley had been decapitated and his head reattached an inch off center.

When Stanley reached the bar, he pushed himself onto a stool and said, "Break out the good stuff, Nick."

Nick nodded solemnly. He grabbed an unlabeled mason jar that contained an elegant corn whiskey distilled by a cousin in Kentucky, poured two shots, turned and set them on the bar.

Stanley tossed back his shot. "I still can't believe it," he said.

"You hear about shit like this on the news. But it only happens to other people," Nick agreed as he refilled Stanley's glass. "Does Dave know?"

"He was with me when the cops came. Which isn't to say he knows."

"I hear you," Nick said somberly. "How's he doing?"

Stanley shrugged and attempted a so-so hand shake. The Parkinson's commandeered the gesture and turned it into a tremor.

Nick nudged Stanley's shot glass closer, then reached for his own. Both men stared uncomfortably at the surface of the bar, pockmarked by years of cigarette burns.

Stanley broke the silence. "The cops said he walked in on a robbery."

"Yeah. So they told me." Nick removed his aviator glasses and set them on the bar. He rubbed his eyes and ran a hand through his wiry hair, still full and red, although gray streaks were infiltrating at the temples. "Poor son of a bitch. Probably a couple of junkies. Panicked, shot and ran."

Stanley raised his glass. "To Pete."

"To Pete," Nick said, raising his.

They clicked their glasses. Nick pointed a remote control at the juke box, launching a Billie Holiday record, and poured another round. "He always liked Billie," Nick said.

"That he did." Stanley picked up the refilled glass. He tried to take a sip but his hand shook so much that whiskey slopped over the edge. Nick grabbed a wet towel and wiped away the spill. From behind, Stanley heard Petra's forced laughter and Billie singing huskily about the difference a day makes.

"Hey!" the accountant shouted. "Where's that cosmo? And bring me some more scotch!"

"Right on it," Nick called back. To Stanley he said quietly, "Guess his mother never taught him to say 'please.' " He poured watered-down vodka and a dash of cranberry juice into a martini glass, grabbed a bottle of cut-rate scotch and carried the drinks to the table. He set the glass before Petra and poured two fingers of scotch into the accountant's empty glass. "Can I get you anything else?" he asked.

"Yeah," the accountant said. "Some real music. Instead of

33

this shit." He flashed the woman a smug smile, so he missed seeing Nick's jaw grind, the anger flare in Nick's eyes and the muscles tensing under Nick's aloha shirt.

"Nick, honey," Petra said quietly. Subtle motions of her eyebrows telegraphed *I can handle this.*

Nick shrugged *Your call* in response. His face relaxed. "This shit," he told the accountant with exaggerated politeness, "is in memory of a good friend of mine. When it's over, feel free to play whatever you want. Fifty cents a song." He reached into a pocket, pulled out two quarters and tossed them on the table. "First one's on me." He pivoted and returned to the bar and threw the wet towel angrily into the sink. "Cigar?" he asked Stanley.

"No, thanks," Stanley said.

Nick reached for the box of cigars and took one for himself. "Didn't I read somewhere tobacco's good for the shakes?" he asked pensively as he ripped off the cellophane wrapper. He lit his cigar, took a relaxed puff and let the smoke drift slowly from his mouth. "I don't know, Stan. This business with Pete. Makes you realize life's too short. Too short to put up with assholes like that," jabbing the cigar in the accountant's direction. "Maybe it's time for me to move on."

"So why don't you? I mean, look at the way the neighborhood's changed. This place must be worth a fortune."

"I do get outrageous offers," Nick admitted. He pushed his glasses to the side and caressed the surface of the bar. "I guess I keep thinking what they'll do to her. Probably strip her down to the bones and turn her into some trendy shithole with wine lists and flowers on the table. Not to mention thirty bucks for an undercooked steak. Enough to make me puke."

"Tear it down and put up condos is more likely. But come on, Nick. It's called progress."

"Right. Progress." Cigar clamped in his teeth, Nick returned the vodka and scotch bottles to the shelves. To the right of the scotch was a photograph of four young men in graduation gowns, mounted in a wood frame with FRIENDS burned into the top and WISCONSIN DELLS burned into the bottom. Nick picked it up, gazed at it for a moment, then set it down. "I keep thinking back to when I met Pete. Got this picture in my mind. Won't go away. Scrawny kid with pimples and a slide rule. You know?"

"That was Pete, all right."

"Smart," Nick said.

"Smartest guy I ever knew," Stanley agreed.

"Knew all the angles. You know how lucky you were to get him to come work for you?"

"Lucky," Stanley repeated listlessly. He stared at the shot glass and turned it in slow circles.

Nick studied Stanley for a moment, then asked, "Something bugging you, Stan? Besides the murder, I mean?"

Stanley peered at Nick over his bifocals. "Did Pete ever tell you he was pissed at me?"

Nick perched the cigar precariously on the edge of the bar and ripped open a bag of pretzels. "Ever's a long time, Stan." He thrust the bag toward Stanley. "Want some?"

Stanley shook his head. "Since the bankruptcy, I mean. Like maybe he thought it was my fault the company went under?"

The Billie Holiday song ended. The accountant scraped his chair against the floor as he rose to go to the jukebox and set matters right.

"Not that I recall," Nick said. "Why?"

"We lost a ton of money, Nick. Dave and Pete and me. When we paid off the creditors."

"So you've told me," Nick's tone implying *ad nauseum.*

A twangy guitar blasted from the jukebox and segued to a nasal voice singing about the joys of driving pickup trucks down country roads.

Stanley said, "It hit me on the drive over. There was something he wasn't telling me. Something he didn't want me to know."

"Well, that could be anything."

"Such as?"

Nick shrugged. "Maybe he had a dress-in-women's-underwear gene. Or a whips-and-chains gene. Who knows?"

" 'Gene'?"

Nick jabbed the cigar at Stanley for emphasis. "I read it somewhere. All our behavior's hard-wired into us by our genes."

"I was thinking something personal," Stanley said. "Having to do with me."

"That's my point. Whatever it was, don't take it personally. Lots of people have things they don't want to talk about." Nick relit his cigar, blew a thick smoke ring at the ceiling, stretched his arm across the counter and tapped cigar ash onto the floor. "Take you, for example."

"What's that supposed to mean?" Stanley asked, reaching for a pretzel. " 'Take me'?"

"Your Ronnie gene."

Stanley dropped the pretzel. "My what?"

"That Ronnie chick who broke your heart in college. The one you spent the last forty years mooning over like a lovesick adolescent? The one you can't get over?"

Nick's comment evoked a parade of images, first Ronnie, then the lovely, bewildered faces of the women Stanley had dated in Ronnie's wake, who became his means of retribution for how Ronnie had treated him. He'd seduce them until they loved him and then drop them. He'd stop calling. He wouldn't take their calls. He'd coldly relish their anxious expressions when they met, act cavalier and dodge their pleas to explain what had gone wrong.

He'd asked Nick for advice about it from time to time, how to purge the toxic fallout from his relationship with Ronnie and cure his need to reject women preemptively. Nick's attitude was, *You are the way you are.* He'd tried therapy. That hadn't helped, either.

There were two problems.

The first was, no woman ever replicated the sheer exhilaration of the sex he'd had with Ronnie. The memory of her lust for games, for toys, for the dark alchemy of transforming pain into pleasure grew more powerful with each passing year. He drew upon it nightly to satisfy him when alone, or as a mental costume to drape over the women in his bed.

No other woman had got him so hard.

The second was that as each new lover grew close to him, the tortured memory of Ronnie's about-face, her abrupt, incomprehensible refusal to continue having sex with him, began to fester. It turned him into something brooding and moody, cold and indifferent.

No other woman had left him so hard.

He sometimes felt he'd been bewitched by Ronnie, and longed for a princess whose kiss could break the spell.

"Like I said, Stan. People have things they don't want to talk about."

"I talk about it with you," Stanley said lamely.

Nick held up his hand. "You know perfectly well what I mean . . ." His voice trailed off as his attention shifted to something behind Stanley. "Just a second," he said, his voice the calm center of a roiling internal fury. He pitched the cigar into the sink.

Stanley turned to look. The accountant had his hand around Petra's wrist. She was struggling to free herself. From her grimace the grip was painful.

Nick came around the bar and strode to the table, carrying a baseball bat. "Closing time," he told the accountant.

"Stay out of this!" the accountant barked, but with faltering bravado as his eyes darted nervously between Nick's face and the bat.

Nick slammed the bat down on the accountant's arm. The accountant shrieked and released Petra. "What the hell you do that for?"

"Because you're treating this fine woman like shit."

"What fine woman?" the accountant asked, incredulous. "She's just a whore, man."

"Get out of here!" Nick said, snarling each word.

Gingerly holding the bruised arm, the accountant stood. "I'm going to report this! To the police!"

"Yeah, you do that. And make sure they send a copy to your wife. Won't she be amused?"

The accountant struggled to pull his overcoat on and started to leave.

Nick swung the bat around and blocked him. "Pay her," he said.

"Pay her?" the accountant asked. "For what? She didn't do anything."

"For wasting her time." He jabbed the bat into the accountant's ample gut. "And you got a tab to settle up."

The accountant looked at Nick, at the woman, at the bat. "Fine," he said angrily. He yanked his wallet from his jacket, pulled out a handful of bills and tossed them on the table. "Worth it not to have to look at her shriveled ass."

Nick swung the bat aside. The accountant stomped out the door.

Petra indifferently separated the bills into denominations. She left two twenties on the table and stuffed the rest in her purse. Nick picked up one of the twenties and tucked it into his shirt pocket. He slid the other back to her.

She snatched it off the table without comment.

"Stick around until we're sure he's gone," Nick said. "Petra. Darling. Where do you find these jerks?"

The woman lit a cigarette and shrugged.

"Don't thank me or anything," Nick said to Petra as he returned to the bar.

"That happen often?" Stanley asked.

"Often enough." Nick leaned the bat against the bar.

"What if he had a gun?"

"If I thought that was a possibility I wouldn't have used a baseball bat."

Stanley watched Petra, reflected in the mirror, smoking sedately as if nothing had happened. "Well, I may or may not have a Ronnie gene. But you, my friend. You've got yourself a whore gene." He started to reach for his shot glass, then hesitated and said, "Damn it!"

"What's wrong?"

"I completely forgot. Mary's cooking dinner tonight."

"Mary?"

"I brought her here a month or so ago. Long brown hair?" He held his hand shoulder-height. "Kind of petite?"

"I remember her," Nick said. "Cute. I just assumed you dumped her already. My God, Stan, this may be a record for you." He winked and added, "What went wrong?"

Stanley shrugged.

"Please don't tell me you've fallen in love."

"The dinner's for our two-month anniversary," Stanley said, evading Nick's question. "Though for the life of me I can't figure out the two-month anniversary of what."

"Well, usually it's how long you been seeing each other. Isn't it?"

"That's the problem," Stanley said. "We've been seeing each other pretty much since last November, when she moved into my building."

"Some friendly advice," Nick said. "You better figure out what happened two months ago before you sit down to eat."

Stanley shook his head helplessly. "I have no clue."

"Stan, you're hopeless." Nick added quietly, "How serious is this?"

"I like her," Stanley said. "But there's so much shit coming down. The bankruptcy auction in May. . . . Now's just not a good time to think about relationships."

"Well, from the way she looked at you when you brought her here, it was obvious she likes you."

"Guess it's true what they say about women our age," Stanley said. "They're so desperate they'll settle for anyone."

Nick retrieved the cigar from the sink, examined it to see if it was salvageable, and relit it. "Don't underestimate yourself."

"Nick," Stanley said quietly. "I'm sixty years old, with no money and a degenerative disease."

"So that's the way you're going to play it?" Nick asked. "You're such a loser that the only people who'd be attracted to you are even bigger losers?" Stanley started to say something, but Nick held his hand up to stop him. "Well, have your pity party, but don't invite me." He shook his head. "Not that the money and the disease have anything to do with it, my friend. You're still a hell of a lot better looking than most men your age. Though a few sit-ups wouldn't hurt. No, you've been this way since I've known you."

"My Ronnie gene, I suppose?" Stanley asked facetiously.

Nick spread his hands. "You said it. I didn't."

"Yeah. Right." Stanley reached for his drink.

Nick grabbed the glass and pulled it away. "No more for you. You're leaving and going to Mary's." He pulled the twenty from his shirt pocket and handed it to Stanley. "And you're going to stop and buy her flowers on the way."

As Stanley was putting on his overcoat, Petra reached out and grabbed at his sleeve.

"You listen to Nick," she said, her eyes bloodshot. "He knows how to treat a lady."

CHAPTER 4

Stanley studied his reflection in his bathroom mirror, with and without bifocals. He exchanged the blazer for a tweed jacket. He went back to the bathroom to make sure his hair was presentable. Satisfied, he rode the elevator down two floors to Mary's apartment.

When Mary opened the door, he handed her a plastic peanut butter jar salvaged from the recycling basket into which he'd dropped in the lilies, still wrapped in cellophane, stems unclipped.

"Flowers!" Mary exclaimed. "And such a lovely vase!" She stepped up on her toes to kiss Stanley and winced. "Oooh! Someone's had a lot to drink."

"Rough day," Stanley muttered.

"Tell me about it over dinner." Mary took the peanut butter jar into the kitchen. She returned with a bottle of Chianti and the lilies, which she'd put in a vase. She placed the flowers on the folding card table she had set with a red tablecloth and candlesticks and gave Stanley the wine. "Sit. Pour," she commanded. She went back to the kitchen and emerged balancing three bowls. "Caesar salad," she announced as she deftly set them down. "No anchovies, sorry. Bow-tie noodles and marinara. Parmesan. I'll serve." Mary was always offering to serve Stanley food, solicitous of the difficulty he had manipulating utensils. She sat, spread her napkin on her lap, and raised her glass in a toast. "Here's to two wonderful months," she said, her eyes twinkling.

Stanley hesitantly raised his glass.

Mary set her glass down, crossed her arms, and looked at him sternly. "You have no idea what I'm talking about, do you?"

Sheepishly, Stanley shrugged. "For the life of me. Did I get drunk and propose, or something?"

She grabbed her wine glass, finished it in one swallow, and poured a refill. "You spent the night. Guess it wasn't as memorable for you as it was for me."

"That was only two months ago? Somehow, seems longer."

"It should have been," Mary said. "You were playing hard to get."

"Was I?" Stanley asked innocently. But he knew she was right and felt his face redden with embarrassment. Whenever they'd get close to having sex, Stanley would begin to shake, or get anxious that he would, and find some excuse to leave. Finally, Mary had flat out asked him if it was the Parkinson's. "Because it doesn't bother me," she'd said. She'd held his left hand, stroked it and added, "Besides, if this is going to vibrate, I can put it to good use."

"As if you didn't know," Mary chided.

"How was your day?" Stanley asked to change the subject.

Mary shrugged. "Uneventful." She sprinkled Parmesan over Stanley's noodles. "Got together with the girls. Read a book. Worked some on the needlepoint." She looked up at Stanley. "You were starting to say about yours?"

"Did I ever mention Pete Tilden?"

"Sure. Your former Jamos Company partner. Before you and Dave went into the detective business."

"I had a visit from the police this afternoon. Pete was murdered."

Mary's face grew ashen. "Oh, my God!" she exclaimed. "How'd it happen?"

"Looks like he came home during a burglary in progress. They shot him."

"That's terrible. You must be in shock."

"Shock," Stanley said, repeating the word as if it was in a foreign language he was trying to understand. He poked his fork listlessly at the noodles. "I guess I should be. Instead, all I feel is paranoid."

"Paranoid about what?"

Stanley took a deep breath. "I stopped at Nick's Bar after I left the office."

"So I noticed."

"The whole way there I couldn't stop thinking that Pete had some secret he was keeping from me. And driving home, I became convinced it was connected to the murder."

"I thought you said he was killed by robbers?"

Stanley sighed. "I'm not saying it makes sense."

"Oh. Now I'm beginning to understand why you say 'paranoid.' "

Stanley tried spearing the noodles with his fork but couldn't get them to stick. "And I also can't shake the feeling I'm being watched."

"Who'd be watching you? Use the big spoon," Mary suggested.

"Today there were two guys on a fire escape across the alley. I was sure they were spying on me."

"You could see them?"

"I just said so. On the fire escape."

"That's my point. If they were really spying on you, wouldn't they hide behind blinds, or something? Why do it from a fire escape, where you could see them?"

"Wouldn't have mattered," Stanley said. "They weren't close enough for me to get a good look at them."

"Then they weren't close enough to get a good look at you

either, were they? Unless—" she held her hands up to her eyes, fingers and thumbs curled to form lenses—"they were using binoculars?"

Stanley shook his head.

"Were they doing anything that struck you as suspicious?"

Stanley shrugged. "Smoking."

"Well," Mary said, "sounds to me like you were spying on them more than they were spying on you."

Stanley moved the noodles to the other side of his plate.

"How long has this been going on?" Mary asked gently. "This feeling you're being watched?"

Stanley shrugged. "In retrospect, seems like months."

"Well!" Mary folded her hands in her lap and sat back. "Let's look at this another way. Assume for the sake of argument that Pete wasn't keeping secrets and you're not being watched. Is there any other reason why you might be prone to paranoia?"

"Could be the new meds I'm on," Stanley speculated. "My doctor warned me that rare side effects include paranoia. And anxiety and hallucinations."

"There you go!" Mary rose and walked around the table and hugged Stanley from behind. "You know what I think? I think you're in shock and the medication is making it worse. You know what else I think? You ought to tell your doctor how you're feeling. Maybe get something to calm you down."

Stanley shut his eyes and focused on the comforting sensation of Mary's arms and the faint smell of her perfume. When she released him he pushed his plate to the side.

"Done?" Mary asked. "You didn't eat much."

"I guess I'm not that hungry."

Mary began stacking the dinner dishes. "Well, I hope you have room for dessert."

Stanley picked up two bowls and followed Mary into the kitchen.

"So how was the detective business today?" Mary asked as she removed a cheesecake from the refrigerator and pulled two plates from a cabinet.

Stanley shrugged. "Dull. Why do you ask?"

Mary glanced at him. "I would think being a detective, exciting things happen all the time. Big piece or small?"

Stanley held up his hand, thumb and forefinger pressed together. He had trained himself to say with a straight face that he and Dave were detectives. Nobody failed to notice Dave's Alzheimer's, so Stanley was used to the information being received with a skeptical look. Some people eventually got up the courage to ask how Dave held up his end. Mary had never asked.

Mary sliced off about a sixth of the cake and put it on Stanley's plate and held it toward him. He accepted the plate with his left hand. The plate shook as he forked off a piece of cheesecake with his right. Chewing reflectively, he said, "If I tell you something, promise you won't tell anyone?"

"Who am I going to tell?"

Stanley set the fork on the plate. "When Jamos Company went under, we lost our health insurance."

"So?"

"So Dave and I have these conditions, and we aren't old enough for Medicare."

"So?"

"You have any idea what health insurance costs if you have Parkinson's or Alzheimer's and you're unemployed?"

"A lot, I imagine."

Stanley took another big bite of cheesecake. "Our insurance agent found a company with an amazingly cheap group rate. Didn't ask about preexisting conditions. It only required one thing. A corporate employer to apply for it."

"So?"

"So that's when we formed Jamos and Mosit."

"Oh," Mary said. "Now I get it. You're not really in business."

"It's not something I advertise," Stanley said.

"I never did get how you could run a detective agency with a partner who's got Alzheimer's. But I didn't think it was my place to ask." After a pensive pause Mary added, "Why bother with the office?"

"Well, we needed a work address. And it gives us somewhere to go during the day. And gives Dave's wife some free time."

"You're saying the insurance is so much cheaper you can afford an office on the difference?"

"I'm saying the insurance is practically unaffordable without it, and the rent's so cheap it hardly matters." Stanley laughed. "You ought to see our office sometime, Mary. It's not exactly the penthouse suite."

"Well, that explains that," Mary said with finality. "But it doesn't explain why you call yourselves detectives, of all things?"

Stanley shrugged. "I get to pretend I'm Humphrey Bogart in *The Maltese Falcon.*"

"Those drugs really do make you hallucinate, don't they?"

"Plus it fits the neighborhood. I mean, nobody would believe us if we said we were selling yachts."

Mary reached for Stanley's plate. "You done or you want more?"

"I'm stuffed," Stanley said, handing her the plate. She put it in the dishwasher. He'd eaten all but a tiny sliver of crust.

Mary put soap in the dishwasher and started it. "Come on into the bedroom. I rented a movie. In honor of our anniversary."

"Hope it's filled with sex," Stanley said.

"It's a romantic comedy." She took his hand and tugged at him to follow. "The sex comes after."

★ ★ ★ ★ ★

MONDAY

★ ★ ★ ★ ★

CHAPTER 5

Stanley stared sullenly at the eggs Tracy had given him a moment before.

The disease was slowly and insidiously sabotaging the manipulative skills Stanley used to feed himself. Lifting food off a plate had become a delicate balancing act even when his hand was steady. Eating solid food with a fork was difficult but possible. Slimy gelatinous food like eggs taunted him. But he had had eggs for breakfast every day before Parkinson's, and refused to let the disease defeat him now.

He made a few futile efforts with a fork, then angrily tossed the fork aside, sandwiched the egg between two pieces of toast and shoved it in his mouth.

"Something wrong?"

Stanley turned at the sound of Tracy from behind. She held a pot of regular. "Need another fork, dear?"

"No," Stanley said, "but can you bring me a couple more pieces of whole wheat? And decaf," he added hastily, pushing the cup away before she could fill it with regular. He and Dave had eaten at Tracy's diner practically daily since they opened their office, but no matter how many times he told her he didn't drink regular, she never got it. He didn't think he owed her the explanation that caffeine exacerbated his tremors.

Plastic pill bottles were lined up by his water glass, a parade of rasagiline, dopamine agonists, co-Q enzyme ten, vitamins, fish oil. He opened them in sequence, washed down the pills he popped in his mouth with tepid decaf, resealed the bottles and put them back in his jacket pocket.

"Where's Dave?" Tracy asked.

Stanley looked at his watch. "Guess he's running late."

"Same thing with Jake. He was out last night. God only knows where," Tracy added. Her cold frown suggested she knew where her husband went, or at least suspected, and didn't approve. "I couldn't get him moving this morning. I can't tell you the number of times I've had to be the waitress, cook, cashier, dishwasher, busboy . . ." She picked up a cup from the adjacent table and filled it with regular. "You mind?" she asked as she sat in the chair across from Stanley.

"Not at all," Stanley said. Mentally he added, *So much for my toast and fresh decaf.*

"You know," Tracy said, looking around at the restaurant, which was empty save for the two of them, "I really thought I had it figured out."

"What figured out?"

"We bought this place because of all the condo conversions. All those loft buildings. It sure looked like it was headed straight this way. That fit right into the plan." She took a healthy slurp of coffee. "The development stopped the day we took title. Should have changed the name from 'Tracy's' to 'Loser's.' "

Stanley decided this was not the best time to comment on the quality of the food. "Markets go in cycles," he said. "It'll turn around."

"Yeah, but in whose lifetime? Meanwhile, we still got our monthly nut, and nobody gets rich flipping pancakes and eggs."

"So what was the plan?" Stanley asked.

Tracy grabbed the regular, refilled her cup and topped off Stanley's before he could stop her. "See how the neighborhood changed. Yuppie, gay, metrosexual, whatever. Then convert this dump to fit in. You know. Upscale. Put paintings on the wall and flowers on the tables. Sell the same shit but serve it with hollandaise sauce and charge ten bucks a plate more." She snorted at the gullibility of the clientele that had never materialized. "And meanwhile this place would become a real gold mine. Shoot up in value. We figured we'd hold on another five, ten years, then sell out and move someplace warm. Like Belize. Or Honduras."

"You ever been there?" Stanley asked.

"Seen pictures," Tracy said.

"Sounds good to me."

Tracy slumped back in the chair and looked up, as if seeking divine counsel. "Yeah, well the current plan is to snap Jake out of his depression. Which I don't see happening until he sees the block go condo." She picked up a napkin, turned away and dabbed at her eye. "Sorry," she said. "I shouldn't get so personal with the customers."

Stanley leaned forward and did his best at a comforting smile. "No apology needed. Dave and I like to think of ourselves as family."

"Thanks." She sniffled and blew her nose. "How's the detective biz?"

"Slow."

Tracy leaned in close, as if to keep what she was about to say out of earshot of the nonexistent other customers. "You know, it's none of my business, but your partner . . . Is he . . . ?" She tapped her finger against her forehead.

"Alzheimer's," Stanley said.

Tracy sat back. "That's what I thought." She mulled that over. "That ever a problem?"

"Not so far."

Tracy took another noisy drink from her cup. "So what brought the two of you to this neck of the woods?"

Stanley shrugged. "The rent. Pure and simple."

"Well, at least this shithole market worked out for one of us. Kept the rent down." She leaned closer. "Any idea how many other tenants in your building?"

"I run into some. The building's far from full, though."

"Jake thinks all the buildings around here are vacant. I said I checked them. There's names on the directories. He said doesn't mean a thing."

"Why were you checking directories?"

Tracy grabbed a napkin and blew her nose. "I had this idea we could print up some flyers and stuff mailboxes. You know. Coupons for free doughnuts, coffee, that sort of thing."

"Sounds like a great idea," Stanley encouraged.

"You do?" Tracy began to sniffle. "From the way Jake reacted, you'd have thought I said, let's take whatever money we got left and burn it." She turned her head and made another pass at her eyes with the tip of the napkin. "Anything I say turns into one more thing we fight about."

The diner door opened, activating a digital rendition of "Jingle Bells." Dave entered, wearing his tan fedora and a beige raincoat. Cindy followed. Her long, straight black hair cascaded over her shoulders. She wore a denim jacket and flattering black slacks. Her clothes taste was simple. She looked good in everything she wore. Each time Stanley saw her he thought, *Dave's a lucky guy.*

Tracy grabbed the coffee pot and rose. "Bring him his usual?"

"And a fresh cup for me," Stanley said. "Decaf," he reminded her back.

Dave picked up a *Sun-Times* from the rack and approached the table, a sheepish grin on his face. He took off his hat and put it on the chair Tracy had just vacated, then took off his overcoat and put it on top of his hat. Cindy watched, dismayed. Before he could sit on both she darted over, snatched them from the chair, put the overcoat on a peg on the wall by the table and rested the hat over the coat. Then she pulled back the chair to help Dave sit.

"Hi, Cindy," Stanley said. "Slow start this morning?"

Cindy held a finger to her lips and beckoned with her hand. Stanley pushed himself off his chair and followed her to the register.

"We had an accident on the way over," Cindy whispered.

Stanley's brow furrowed with concern. "Anybody hurt?"

"Only the leather. Assuming urine hurts it."

"Oh. That kind."

Cindy sighed. "Frankly, I wish it was the other." She looked over Stanley's shoulder at Dave to make sure he was out of earshot. "I guess it's time for adult diapers, but I just can't bear the thought of it."

"I wish there was something I could say," Stanley said.

Cindy shrugged. "It is what it is. Just be careful if you have to drive him somewhere. Put a towel on the car seat."

"Where would we have to drive?" Stanley asked.

"God, Stan. I don't know what I'd do if it weren't for you."

"You know Pete's funeral's on Thursday?"

"Nick told me. Stan, I am so sorry about that. I know how close you were."

"How's Dave taking it?"

"I don't know. He came home Friday and told me something bad happened to Pete. He didn't remember what. I couldn't reach you, so I called Nick, who told me what happened. Then this morning Dave asked me if Pete was okay." Tears began to well in her eyes.

Stanley put a hand on her shoulder. "Go," he said. "See you at five." He watched her leave to the tune of "Jingle Bells."

When Stanley returned to the table, Dave's newspaper was opened to a full-page photograph. Dave placed his index finger on the caption and read it out loud, giving each word an inflection inconsistent with the context. Stanley was spared further recitation by Tracy's setting Dave's plate of pancakes on the table.

"Jingle Bells" played again.

Tracy said, "Hot damn," under her breath as two men entered. Each wore a brown Italian leather jacket over jeans.

Stanley figured the jackets at easily a thousand each.

Both men had full heads of hair. One's was white and combed straight back, the other's was black and glistened with oil. White hair had a beefy face, pockmarked and grim. Black hair was his junior by at least twenty years. A small green duffel bag hung from his shoulder.

Stanley kept staring at the men, trying to understand why they seemed familiar, until the older one looked at Stanley and locked eyes, clearly annoyed. He detached himself from the younger, strode chest out to Stanley and said, "Can I help you?"

"Sorry?"

"You was looking at me like I wasn't wearing pants or something. There some problem?"

Stanley was about to offer a perfunctory apology when he figured it out. "Wait a second. You two work around the corner? I think I saw you on the fire escape last Friday."

"That a crime?"

The younger man came over, set the duffel bag on the floor and put a hand on the older man's shoulder. "Come on, Dad. Have some coffee. Let them eat their breakfast." He nodded at Stanley. "Don't mind my dad. He wakes up on the wrong side of the bed every morning. Don't think his bed has a right side."

"I have a bed," Dave said.

"Good for you," the older man growled.

Dave looked quizzically at Stanley. "Is it time for bed already?"

Tracy walked over with her coffeepots. "The four of you

together?" she asked.

"No!" the older man snapped.

"We'll eat over there," the younger man said, pointing to the farthest booth. "Name's Tim," he said to Stanley, extending a hand.

Stanley shook it. "I'm Stanley. This is Dave."

Tim shook Dave's hand. "This here's my dad, Doug." He turned to Doug. "You think you can say hello?"

Doug scowled.

Tim winked at Stanley. "He'll be okay when he gets his coffee. Come on, Dad," he said, grabbing the duffel bag and guiding Doug toward the booth. "Time for breakfast." As he walked away he turned to Tracy and beckoned her to follow. "We'll need that caffeine ASAP."

"Who was that?" Dave asked.

"Beats me. You mind?" Stanley asked as he pulled over Dave's newspaper, less out of interest in it than to remove a distraction from Dave's finishing breakfast. He opened it to the sports section and began to read with indifference. Tracy walked by, carrying two menus. He heard her tell Doug and Tim, "I'll give you a couple of minutes." She walked back and disappeared into the kitchen.

A moment later Stanley heard a scrape on the floor behind him. He turned to look as Tim pulled over a chair from the adjacent table and straddled it, holding a menu.

"You two regulars here?" Tim asked.

"We come here often enough."

Tim glanced at the kitchen door to make sure Tracy hadn't emerged. He dropped his voice and said, "Thing is, me and Dad usually eat breakfast over on Roosevelt. Only been here once before, right after it opened. Food was so bad, Dad practically puked. Said he'd never come back. Except this morning our regular place had a fire, and looks of it, it ain't reopening so soon. So I says to Dad, let's give that place around the corner another shot. Dad didn't speak to me the rest of the way here. That's part of the reason for his shitty mood."

"I hadn't noticed," Stanley said.

"Anyway, you two got that 'regulars' look, and I figured . . . I mean, I realize this ain't haute cuisine"—pronouncing the word *haughty*—"but you probably know what's good." He opened the menu and held it toward Dave.

Stanley intercepted it. "We're not what you'd call adventurous. Dave here's a pancakes man. Dave, what do you think of the pancakes?"

"Good," Dave said.

"I'm as boring. Fried eggs sunny side up and whole wheat."

Tim shrugged. "Can't go wrong with that."

"Now, if I was a risk taker, I'd try the *Chef Recommends.*" Stanley read from the menu, "One egg sunny side up on whole wheat toast with sausage patty, smothered in nacho cheese and sliced jalapenos." He handed the menu back to Tim.

"Sounds right up Dad's alley. Thanks." As Tim rose he added, "Just hope Dad doesn't get the heaves."

Ten minutes later Tracy passed, balancing two plates on a tray. Stanley looked at his watch. He looked at Dave's plate. Less than half of the pancakes were gone. He started reading an article about the White Sox's prospects for the coming season. Tracy walked by, replacing his coffee cup with a fresh cup of regular as she did. He shoved the cup away and resumed reading the paper. He felt a tap on his shoulder. He turned. Tim was standing behind his chair, beckoning. "Can you come over for a minute?"

"Sure," Stanley said, folding the newspaper. As he rose, he told Dave, "Finish up."

Tim sat, speared a wad of pancakes with one hand and gestured toward the space next to Doug with the other. "Have a seat," he said as he stuffed the pancakes in his mouth.

Stanley slid in and asked, "What's up?"

Doug shoved away his plate, oily from the residue of the *Chef Recommends*. "Your friend," he said, nodding over his shoulder in Dave's direction. "It's none of my business, but . . . Alzheimer's?"

Stanley nodded. "Right. On both counts."

Tim shook his head sadly. "That's rough, man. Reason Dad asks, my grandma—his mother—had it. Sharp as a tack back in her day. Hell of a way to go." He took a sip of coffee. "Man, you know what I remember? What the doc told us after the diagnosis. He said, when she's at the point where you think she's ninety percent there and ten percent gone, what you got to understand is, she's ten percent there and ninety percent gone. Didn't believe him."

"I'm not so sure I agree, either," Stanley said.

Tim jabbed his fork at Stanley. "But he was right. Last thing to go was the small talk. She was on autopilot, man. I remember once we was walking down the street and she sees some wino in an alley, babbling to himself and stinking of piss. She walks up to him and starts up with, 'This here's my grandson.' Had no idea who she was talking to. Just making small talk." He shook his head again. "Autopilot." He reached across the table and clapped Stanley's shoulder. "Anyway, that's why we asked. 'Cause once you know the signs . . ."

"Got it," Stanley said.

Doug affected a cough. "Hey, sorry for coming on so hard before," he said. "I'm no damn good before breakfast." He extended a hand.

Stanley shook Doug's hand and said, "No problem."

"You new to the 'hood?"

Stanley shrugged. "We been here a while. In the building

next door. So was that the two of you I saw on the fire escape last week?"

"Smoking?"

Stanley nodded.

"Could have been." Doug speared the last of the *Chef Recommends*. "Got to go outside for a smoke. Getting to the point you won't be able to take a piss in the city no more. I tell you, Chicago's got more ordinances than people." He shoved the food in his mouth. "What business you in? If you don't mind my asking?"

"Private investigation."

Tim's eyebrows arched. "Detective? You shitting me?"

"No shit," Stanley said.

"Well, good for you," Doug said. "You got a card? You never know when someone will need a detective."

Stanley felt himself on the verge of stammering. It had never occurred to him to print cards, any more than it would have to print brochures or have a website. The last thing he expected was to be asked to provide investigative services. He made a show of taking out his wallet and inspecting its compartments. "Guess not," he said, and quickly added, "What about you fellows?"

Tim patted his lips with the tip of the napkin. "We got ourselves a real sweet operation."

"What you call your niche business," Doug interjected.

Tim leaned in close and his voice dropped. "Let's say you're married. But you got a little number on the side. You want to get her a present but don't want no record of it. No cash withdrawal. No check. No credit card bill. You see the problem? So let's say the wife's got a nice piece. Well, one day it disappears. What happened to it? Who knows? Meanwhile, you bring it to us. We strip it down. Sell the pearls and the rocks and the gold. Take the bread and buy your babe a trinket. No record.

Nobody the wiser." He leaned back and grinned. "Sweet, huh?"

"And legal," Doug added.

"What about the insurance companies?"

"We got that angle covered, man. Get this. Our deal with the clients is, they can't file a police report. Got to sign a paper commissioning us to sell the goods for them. That's in case someone comes around accusing us of fencing stolen merchandise. Otherwise, the paper don't see light of day."

"And no police report means no insurance claim," Doug added.

"Of course, hubby's got to persuade the wife not to file one." Tim laughed. "We've had a couple of those. The insurance company came sniffing around because the wife filed a claim. We showed them the paper. They caught on real quick. Sure would have liked to be there when the shit hit the fan." He winked at Stanley. "So what do you think?"

"Sounds like you got yourself a nice setup," Stanley said. He started to edge out of the booth. "Excuse me. I shouldn't leave Dave by himself."

Tim's hand came down on Stanley's arm. Stanley could feel the power in the grip. Tim wasn't forcing him to stay, but wasn't exactly giving him permission to leave, either. "Reason I'm telling you is, our business is all word of mouth."

Stanley nodded, then looked down at Tim's hand clamping his arm.

"Figure in your line of work, you might meet people who can use our services. And we're real generous with referral fees. Even throw a few cases your way." He winked and released his grip.

"I'll keep it in mind," Stanley said, edging a few more inches toward the end of the booth.

"Long as we're on that subject, how's your friend hold up his end of the business?" Tim asked.

Stanley fought the reflexive urge to say, *What business?* He shrugged, stood and said noncommittally, "He's got his good days and his bad days. But don't we all."

"Well, Dad here's got his bad days and his worse days." He turned to Doug and said, "You ever get Alzheimer's, man, you're out the door." He turned back to Stanley and clapped him on the arm. "You're a saint, man. Just remember that when you go. In case they make a mistake and don't drop you off at the pearly gates." He raised a hand and flagged Tracy. "Check, honey," he called. He stretched and added, "Back to the salt mines."

Doug sidled out of the booth and walked over to the cash register, pulling an inch-thick roll of bills from his pocket on the way. Tim stopped at Stanley's table, put a hand on Dave's shoulder and asked, "How you doing, buddy?"

Dave looked up from the *Sun-Times* and flashed Tim a smile.

"Looking good for the Sox this season?"

Dave grinned and stabbed an index finger at the photograph on the back page.

Tim looked at Stanley and rolled his eyes. Then he turned to Dave and said, "That's right, buddy. The White Sox."

"Come on, Dave," Stanley said, picking up the paper. "Time to go to work."

"Do we still work at Jamos Company?" Dave asked, looking suddenly confused.

The opening riff to "Surfin' USA" sounded from Stanley's pants pocket. He extracted his cell phone and checked the caller ID. A number with a three-ten area code. *Probably another wrong number,* he thought. He flipped it open and said, "Hello?"

"Is this Stanny Jamos?"

Only two people had ever called him Stanny. One was his mother. After he broke up with the other, he was emphatic that nobody was to call him that again. His heart began to race. His tongue felt tied up in knots. He doubted he could do more than stammer. He said nothing.

"Stanny? It's Ronnie. Dumat."

The name was unnecessary. Stanley recognized the voice as clearly as if it had been forty years ago. His lips moved reflexively, soundlessly, disconnected from a brain too flabbergasted to engage in normal conversation. He finally forced himself to say, "Ronnie?"

"Listen, Stanny," Ronnie said, "I know this is out of the blue, but the fact is . . . damn! Stanny, I really need to see you!"

Her urgency alarmed him. He asked, "Are you okay?"

"I'm fine. It's complicated. Can you meet me?"

"Where are you? What's wrong?"

"I'm . . ." Her words were drowned out by the shrill bark of a voice over a loudspeaker. "That's my flight. I'll be in Chicago this afternoon. Let me check into the hotel and freshen up and we'll meet for dinner. Okay? My treat."

"Can't you give me even a hint?"

She named a River North restaurant. "I'll make it for six. We'll beat the crowd. I'll explain everything. I got to go," she added, sounding winded, and disconnected.

"How will we recognize each other?" Stanley asked the dead line.

CHAPTER 6

Stanley knew something wasn't right the minute he and Dave entered the diner. It took him a moment to identify it.

No "Jingle Bells."

No lights on, either.

From the kitchen an angry male voice shouted, "It's just a switch, you bitch!"

A second male voice laughed, repeated, "Switch, you bitch," in a Mexican accent, and laughed again.

The red LEDs on the coffee warmers came on, followed by flickering overhead as the fluorescents lit up.

Stanley heard Tracy warn, "I mean it, Jake. Don't," as the kitchen door banged open and Tracy came through walking backwards, holding a long spatula like a bat. She was unaware that Stanley and Dave were standing by the cash register until she turned around. Seeing them, she gasped and dropped the spatula.

Stanley whispered, "You okay?"

Tracy took a deep breath. "Overloaded a circuit," she said quietly and attempted a smile.

Stanley nodded toward the kitchen door. "Jake?"

Tracy put a finger over her lips. "I told him before about that outlet. He gets angry if I correct him about anything."

Stanley walked back to the diner door, opened it, activating "Jingle Bells," and said in a loud voice, "Hi, Tracy. What's for lunch?" Then he whispered, "At least he knows someone's here."

He put a hand on Dave's back and gave him a gentle push. "Come on, Dave. Let's grab a table."

"The usual?" Tracy asked.

"Hamburger," Dave said.

"Make that two," Stanley said. "Mine well done, please." His voice dropped. "Jake gives you any trouble, I'm calling nine-one-one."

Stanley removed his overcoat and draped it over a chair. As they sat, Dave said, "She doesn't look all right, Stanley."

"You noticed that, did you?"

Dave removed his hat and put it on the table over the napkin dispenser. "You don't, either."

Stanley moved the hat to an adjacent table. "I'm a little rattled, Dave."

"Why, Stanley?"

"You remember Ronnie Dumat?"

Dave struggled to concentrate. He shook his head sideways. "But my memory's not so good."

"My girlfriend from college?"

Dave shrugged. "Pictures sometimes help me remember, Stanley."

"Anyway, she called me this morning. I haven't talked to her since . . ." *That day,* he thought. He forced a smile. "Since college. All of a sudden she has to see me. Funny."

"Funny, Stanley?"

"Last week Pete leaves my life for good. Today Ronnie re-enters it. Some coincidence, huh?"

"Stanley?"

"Yeah, Dave?"

"Did something bad happen to Pete?"

Stanley was about to answer when "Jingle Bells" intruded. He looked up. Birkholz and Hustad walked in. They immediately spotted Stanley and Dave. It wasn't difficult, with no other customers in the diner. "Good call," Birkholz's voice boomed as they strode quickly to the table and pulled out the other two chairs. "Went to your office but you weren't there. Hustad here says, 'Bet they're having lunch at the diner next door.' " He looked around for an ashtray. Finding none, he rested his cigarette on the rim of a saucer.

"We talked to your lawyer late Friday afternoon. Anna Nelson. Nice woman," Hustad said, easing himself into a chair. "Look, sorry to interrupt, but she told us some things. Raised a few questions. You mind?"

"Not at all," Stanley said. "Join us for lunch?"

"Why not?" Hustad pulled his notepad from his jacket pocket and began flipping through the pages.

"Nothing for me," Birkholz said, patting his belly. "Doctor's orders."

Stanley looked at Birkholz over the rim of his bifocals. "What does your doctor say about cigarettes?"

Birkholz looked sidelong at Stanley as he knocked cigarette ash into the saucer. "He says they won't give me the shakes, is what."

"Come on, Chris," Hustad said, frowning.

The kitchen door banged open. Tracy came through, balancing a tray. The sound of men talking in Spanish in the kitchen muted when the door swung shut.

As Tracy set Stanley's and Dave's hamburgers on the table, she admonished Birkholz, "Please don't smoke in here, sir. I'm worried about getting cited."

"So call a cop," Birkholz said. He pulled his jacket back, revealing the badge over his breast pocket.

Hustad looked at Tracy and smiled. It made his eyes look even sadder. "I'd like a hamburger, ma'am. Please."

"Ma'am," Tracy repeated wistfully. "Please. Well, aren't you a gentleman."

"And a ginger ale," Hustad added. As Tracy left the table, he studied his notes. "We asked Ms. Nelson if she had any idea why someone might want to kill Mr. Tilden. She said she didn't. But she did say he'd been acting strange lately. Uncooperative." He looked up from his notepad. "Would you concur?"

"If Pete was acting strange, it's news to me," Stanley said, pounding the bottom of the catsup bottle.

"She left us a voice mail this morning. Said Mr. Tilden carried around millions of dollars he won in games. Something like that. Said maybe we should look into it. Said you could explain it."

"So here we are," Birkholz said. "What was he? A gambler?"

Hustad pulled out a ballpoint pen and poised to write.

"It wasn't money. It was prizes," Stanley said through a mouthful of hamburger. "And he hardly 'carried them around.' It was only on rare occasions. And he didn't win them. And they weren't his games."

"Then whose games were they?" Hustad asked, writing furiously.

"Our clients'. That's the business Jamos Company was in. Expediting games. And contests."

Hustad looked up from the notepad. "You want to run that by me again? In English this time?"

Gripping the hamburger in his steady right hand, Stanley said, "You know how big companies—gas, soft drinks, fast food—run contests and games? Like the ones with prizes printed under bottle caps or cards handed out with the burgers?"

Hustad nodded. "Sure."

"That was our business. We placed the winning bottle caps on the bottles and distributed the game cards and reviewed the prize submissions. I ran sales and program design. Dave was finance. And Pete was implementation."

"I see," Hustad said.

"I don't," Birkholz said. "What does that have to do with these millions of dollars your lawyer talked about?"

"That's what I meant by implementation," Stanley said. "Here's an example. You remember *Bottle Blastoff?*"

Hustad snapped his fingers to jog his memory. "Some soft drink, wasn't it? The bottle caps had pictures of astronomical objects, planets and such?"

"And some were worth serious money. The top prize was a million dollars. Won, as I recall, by an artist from Paducah who gave it all to her ashram. But that's beside the point. How do you think it got to a grocery store in Kentucky?"

Hustad shrugged.

"Well, first of all, someone had to set aside a few thousand bottle caps and then supervise while the insides were overprinted with prizes. Then someone had to take those bottle caps to the bottlers, and stand by while they went on bottles, and see them out the door. That someone was Pete." Stanley took another bite out of his hamburger.

Birkholz reached across the table and plucked a fry from Dave's plate. "That was Mr. Tilden's job?"

"Part of it." Stanley returned the hamburger to his plate and leaned forward, eager to explain, to be speaking about Jamos Company as a living entity rather than a collection of assets to be auctioned. "He also designed the technology to make the system work. And verified that prize submissions were genuine."

"Maybe I'm dense," Birkholz said, "but why wouldn't the soft drink company just do that itself? What did they need you for?"

"Lots of reasons. Because running contests isn't their business. Because they don't have the know-how or talent to do it right. Because even if they did, we did it better. And it gave them someone to blame if anything went wrong. I mean, can you imagine the nightmare if there were problems with the bottle caps and the soft drink company had caused them?"

"Problems?" Hustad asked and jotted something in his notepad. "What sorts of problems?"

"Well, for starters, think about what happens if the prizes don't get randomly distributed."

"I'm thinking," Birkholz said. "I'm just not understanding."

"There were only a few winning bottle caps. You don't want them all turning up in Paducah. That may sound easy. But in fact it's very complicated."

"Any other problems?" Hustad asked.

"Sure. Verification. Specifically, making sure that submissions were genuine. You know? Weeding out the counterfeits." Stanley stuffed the last of his hamburger in his mouth.

Tracy approached the table, set a hamburger and a ginger ale before Hustad and asked, "Everything okay?"

Dave gave her a thumbs-up.

"Run this thing with the bottle caps by me again," Birkholz asked. "Because I remember Bottle Blastoff. And every bottle I opened said, 'You lose,' or something like that."

"Probably, 'Sorry, play again.' "

"Whatever." Birkholz took a handful of fries from Hustad's plate and dipped them in Dave's catsup. "You telling me he put all those 'You lose' caps on the bottles?"

"He's saying he put the prize winners on the bottles," Hustad corrected.

"By himself?" Birkholz crushed out his cigarette on the saucer, reached across the table and tore off a chunk of Hustad's hamburger.

"Not by hand, if that's what you mean." Stanley picked up a fry and nibbled at it. "Pete would feed each bottle cap into the bottling machine and then watch it get stamped on. That way he knew which bottles had specific caps. And he also knew which cases the bottles went into. What trucks they went on. What distributors the trucks delivered to. What locations they served. So if, say, a million-dollar prize was targeted to Southern California and a claim was submitted by someone in New Jersey, unless there was a real good explanation he'd know it was probably a fake."

"I don't know," Birkholz said, grabbing another handful of fries from Hustad's plate. "If the bottler knows Mr. Tilden's showing up with the million-dollar winner, doesn't sound all that secure to me."

"That's not how it worked," Stanley said. "First of all, there were several bottlers, and the big prizes could have gone to any of them. And second, Pete didn't show up announcing, 'Here's the big one, and I'm putting it on this bottle.' He and his crew would come with cases of bottle caps, which they'd place on bottles. But the important thing was, the bottler had no idea if there were any winners in there or if so, how big. And in fact most of the caps Pete brought said, 'Sorry, play again.' And Pete wouldn't leave until all the bottles were loaded on the trucks and the trucks were on the road."

"You make it sound like nothing could go wrong."

"Nothing could," Stanley said. "And nothing ever did."

"Except Mr. Tilden was murdered," Hustad said. "And where there's big money, there's big motive. Tell me about the counterfeits."

"We'd get them every so often."

"When you say 'we,' " Hustad said, writing, "who do you mean?"

"I mean us. Jamos Company."

"How did they get to you?" Birkholz asked. "My neighbor won a couple of twelve-packs, and I'm pretty sure he went back to the grocery store to pick them up."

"Sure," Stanley said. "To redeem the small prizes, free soft drinks up to, say, five bucks, the customer could go to pretty much any retailer. For the bigger prizes, the claimants had to send their bottle caps to a post office box. That was us. Pete would collect the letters and bring them to our warehouse. He had a special place, called the verification room, where each letter was opened. You practically needed a top secret security clearance to get inside it. Pete and Dave and I were the only ones who knew the access code. That's where he'd find out if the bottle cap was legit. If it was, we'd authorize the prize." Stanley suppressed a smile and thought, *The good old days.*

Birkholz tore off another piece of Hustad's hamburger, lit a cigarette and extinguished the match in the catsup on Dave's plate. Simultaneously chewing and taking a drag on his cigarette, he asked, "How would you know if it was a fake?"

"It was Pete's job to know."

"But how?"

Stanley shook his head. "That's proprietary. Let's just say the prizes were coded."

Birkholz shrugged. "So say you got a fake. What would you do?"

"Send a polite letter explaining that the bottle cap we received was not genuine," Stanley explained. "Apologize for the inconvenience. Enclose a coupon for a free twelve-pack."

"You sent that to someone who was trying to steal from you?" Birkholz asked, indignant.

"And what would you do?"

"It's a federal crime," Birkholz said. "Involving the U.S. Mail."

"You're thinking like a law enforcement officer, not a businessman. What's the person who submitted it going to say? He found it on the street. Any way the publicity comes out would only be bad. And in any case, that was the soft drink company's call, not ours."

"I can imagine getting a letter saying you sent us a fake could make Mr. Tilden some enemies," Birkholz said. "Did he ever get threats of retaliation?"

"The letters weren't on our letterhead," Stanley said. "We used the client's stationery, and signed with a fictitious name. The public didn't even know we existed."

"Scratch that," Birkholz said. He tugged absently at the ends of his mustache, then took another drag on his cigarette. "You got anything else?" he asked Hustad.

Hustad tapped his pen against his notepad. "What would Mr. Tilden have done if he found out that someone had been stealing prizes?"

"I never heard of that happening," Stanley said. "But if it did, he wouldn't have confronted the thief. He would have just told the client about it."

"Then what about the opposite? What if Mr. Tilden kept the winning prize for himself?"

Stanley shook his head. "Pete was disqualified from winning any prizes. We all were. But even if he did, I can't believe someone would kill him for it. And why now? You're talking about events that would have happened years ago. Before Jamos Company went out of business."

Hustad closed his notepad and put it in his jacket. "Well, guess that's it," he said. "All we got are dead ends. What we need is a lead."

From where they sat, it sounded like a stack of dishes tumbled and shattered. Hustad's head jerked in the direction of the kitchen. Birkholz turned slowly, curiosity trumping his indifference. They heard Tracy's plaintive, "Please, Jake," and then, louder and agitated, "Raul, stop him!"

"Hey, mano," a loud Mexican voice cautioned.

Another male voice spat out, "Bitch."

Hustad started out of his chair, reaching inside his jacket for his holstered gun. He froze in a crouch, waiting for something else to happen. Nothing did for ten, twenty seconds. Then a car engine roared and tires squealed. A moment later Tracy came through the kitchen door, paused at the register, grabbed the tab and walked slowly to the table, eyes downcast.

Hustad sat and asked, "Everything okay, ma'am?"

Tracy placed the tab face down before Stanley, muttered something about enjoying lunch, turned and walked away. She didn't seem to notice that Hustad held a gun.

Birkholz grinned. "Looks to me like she could use some new help."

"It's her husband," Stanley said quietly.

"Put your gun away," Birkholz told Hustad. He turned to Stanley. "Domestic violence ain't our jurisdiction," he said, putting out his cigarette in the catsup on Dave's plate. "Shame he didn't kill her. Then we could have done something about it." He rose, put on his overcoat and said, "Thanks for lunch," as he headed toward the door.

Hustad reminded Stanley of a sad old basset hound as he handed Stanley a ten for the hamburger and ginger ale and shrugged as if to say, *Our partners don't always turn out the way we want. Something you probably understand.*

CHAPTER 7

Ronnie had picked a hot restaurant. When Stanley arrived at six twenty, the wait without a reservation was already ninety minutes.

The arrival time was deliberate. Stanley had calculated twenty minutes to be enough time for Ronnie to get there first without thinking him unacceptably late. But the hostess said she hadn't checked in and refused to seat him until Ronnie showed. "Why don't you wait at the bar?" she said. It was not an invitation but an expression of Stanley's irrelevance, her desire that he go somewhere else. She uttered the question mechanically while staring at a plastic seating chart, her hand hovering over it with a felt-tipped marker, engrossed in solving some logistical problem.

Stanley reflected on the answers. *Because it's painfully loud in there. Because there's nowhere to sit. Because I resent your indifference.* But he knew the hostess wouldn't care; the confrontation would make his arm start flapping like the wings of a decapitated chicken, and it just wasn't worth it.

When I was entertaining Jamos Company clients I would have palmed her a fifty and gotten whatever table I wanted, he thought.

Stanley's hand began to shake. He went to the bathroom for some water to wash down an anti-tremor pill. As he stood over the sink, cold water running, he stared at the person in the mirror staring back at him. *When did you become sixty?* he asked himself. He used to flatter himself that he had a youthful appearance. He still had most of his hair, most of which was still brown. The reflection seemed to reverse that, like a photographic negative, highlighting the gray streaks. He wondered if Ronnie would recognize him.

He knew he'd recognize her.

He wondered if the chemistry would still be there.

He wondered if she still had the same delicious proclivities.

He thought, *Who the hell are you kidding?*

Before leaving the bathroom he rechecked his outfit.

He approved of the jacket, even though a sweater would have been better at hiding the gut. A jacket was always the right choice.

The black slacks were too tight, but the only real option. Before the diagnosis, Stanley's waistline had been a firm thirty four. With increased alcohol consumption and decreased exercise, he quickly outgrew his clothes. At thirty seven inches, he bought new jeans and the black slacks. An inch and a half later he added khakis. He would have been more comfortable in the khakis, but in March in Chicago that was out of the question.

He'd debated oxfords versus loafers. Although the muscular control of his fingers had degenerated to the point where his handwriting was an illegible scrawl, he could still tie shoelaces. But shoes with laces were too formal, and he was hoping for anything but formal.

The rule he'd learned from his father was simple: Dress for success. His only uncertainty was the success for which he was dressing.

He didn't see her when he returned from the bathroom. He looked at his watch. Six twenty-nine. The meter was coming close to crossing from *acceptably late* into the red *inconsiderate* zone.

He ordered a glass of bourbon and carried it to a bench by

the door. Taking a sip he wondered, *Had Ronnie been prone to showing up late?*

He couldn't remember.

No surprise. Since her call he'd been trying to reconstruct their time together, only to discover how few details he could recall.

He remembered being introduced to her in the fall of his senior year, but no memory of where, or by whom. He remembered distinctly what came next. She asked him out. They went to a movie. When it was over she brought him to her apartment. She took him to her bed, no embarrassment, no explanation, the most natural thing in the world. What she did that night, how she looked, was amazing, everything he'd fantasized about. He lost his equilibrium to her. He never recovered it.

What came after was blurry.

Was Ronnie ever at the frat house? He had no memories of that. Maybe she didn't like the toga parties and other drunken brawls they were notorious for throwing.

He sensed he'd spent a lot of time at Ronnie's apartment. He had an image of it, fancier than was typical for a University of Wisconsin student, but not everybody was into spartan living. She had a pretty roommate who was seldom around, always going out to parties, always dressed sexy. He couldn't remember her name.

Ronnie must have known Dave and Pete and Nick, but he couldn't remember what they'd thought of her back then. All the other minutiae of their time together, what he'd done with Ronnie, the places they'd gone together, had evaporated. All except the sex. That memory was indelible. It had molded his mind, transforming the Ronnie who inhabited it into the standard by which each and every subsequent woman was judged and found wanting. The thought of it made him tingle.

It made him think that if she showed any interest . . . and if he didn't have this disease . . .

Stanley was staring at a strikingly beautiful woman of undecipherable racial heritage when he felt a hand on his shoulder. In the periphery of his vision he saw fingertips with red nails and nicotine stains. A head descended. The hair was glossy and black, cut shoulder length and parted on the right. The face matched the mental image, albeit distorted by alien red lipstick and a uniform glossiness that could only have come from a bottle. The body followed, descending gracefully until it was seated, her hips touching his, dressed in a sleeveless white blouse and a tight black skirt that stopped inches above the knees, emphasizing her still-shapely black-stockinged legs. His reflexive reaction was, *Chicago women don't look like this. Not at this age.* It was a body of someone whose life is spent outdoors year round, with trainers and meticulous dietary regimens and, probably, surgical intervention. It was a body sculpted to navigate Hollywood.

"Stanny," she said, staring deeply into his eyes. "You haven't changed a bit." Her breath smelled of mint and tobacco.

"Bullshit," he said.

He extended his hand.

Ronnie pushed it away, leaned forward and kissed him delicately on the lips. "Have you been waiting long?" she asked as she pulled a pack of cigarettes from her purse and tapped out a cigarette.

"You can't smoke in here," Stanley cautioned.

Ronnie's eyes flared with anger under eyebrows that, he observed, were defined with black eyeliner. "You're serious?"

"Look around. You see anyone smoking?"

"Damn!" Ronnie closed her eyes and inhaled deeply, as if about to begin some Yogic exercise. It made her breasts jut forward.

The sight tickled Stanley's memory. He forced his eyes not to drift below her neck.

"What about in the bar?"

"Have to go outside," Stanley said.

"Will you come with me?" Ronnie asked, sounding almost childlike. She stood, but as she did the hostess approached, seating chart in hand, and asked, "Dumat party?"

Ronnie nodded. "Do I have time to go outside for a smoke first?" she asked urgently.

"I can't hold your table," the hostess said. "I can put you back on the list, but there's a two-hour wait."

"Damn!"

The hostess shrugged indifferently, said, "This way," and turned.

Stanley let Ronnie go ahead of him so he could observe her from the rear. She hadn't lost her easy gait, sexy in her unself-consciousness. She still caused heads to turn.

The hostess left them at their table with two menus, and a wine list that Ronnie grabbed aggressively. "We're well past formalities, aren't we? The lady must defer to the gentleman to order the wine and all that crap? Besides, I'm the one from wine country. And besides that, this is my expense account, not yours."

"Expense account?"

"In due time."

A waitress arrived as Ronnie was talking. She attempted to interrupt and deliver the routine, tell Stanley and Ronnie her name and that she would be serving them and inquire with disinterest masked by an unctuous solicitousness how they were doing tonight. Without taking her eyes off Stanley, Ronnie blocked the effort with a curt raise of the hand. "The red zin, please. Number one twenty-nine. We'll order appetizers when you get back. You'll love it, Stanny. Assuming you're not one of those sixties holdouts who haven't made the switch to wine from . . ." She put a thumb and index finger up to pursed lips and made a loud inhaling sound.

"Bourbon, actually," Stanley said, lifting his glass as if to prove the point. He didn't add that red wine was occasionally incompatible with the dopamine agonists. "A sin I learned from Nick Fitzgerald. If you remember him."

"Of course I remember Nick. How's he doing?"

"Great."

Ronnie leaned back a few inches as if to get a better view of him. "I meant what I said, Stanny. You haven't changed a bit."

"And I meant what I said. Bullshit."

She waved away his comment. "Don't get me wrong. I mean the real you. The inner you. The aura. It's still the same."

Stanley reflected on this. "California bullshit!" he laughed. "But you. You look the same as you did in college. And I'm not talking aura, either."

"You're sweet to say that," Ronnie said with a lopsided grin. The sight of it jerked his memory, like a dog yanking on a leash upon catching the scent of a bitch in heat. Her otherwise even smile became lopsided after an orgasm. She spread her napkin on her lap and propped her elbows on the table and rested her chin on her interlaced fingers. "It's really good to see you again, Stanny."

"It's good to see you again, too, Ronnie."

She stared at him, smiling, silent, her eyes locked onto his, unblinking.

Stanley couldn't look away. He felt the awkwardness intensify like the whistle of an approaching freight train. He fought the urge to avert her stare, to hear anything, no matter how stupid or trite, come from his mouth to fill the vacuum.

He was on the verge of yielding when she said, "So you're thinking. How do we cut the crap?"

Stanley felt release. Like learning he had passed a test he'd feared he'd failed. "Something like that."

"Well, if old lovers can't cut through crap, then what's the use of being old lovers? Right?"

Stanley raised his bourbon glass in a mock toast.

The waitress stopped by with a bottle, uncorked it and poured Ronnie a taste. Ronnie swirled the glass, brought it to her nose, inhaled and set the glass down with a nod, all the while keeping her gaze riveted on Stanley's eyes. The waitress poured two glasses and inquired about appetizers.

"What are your two best," Ronnie asked without looking up, "that don't have farm-raised fish or hormone-fed animals?"

"Well, there's . . ."

"Whatever they are, that's what we'll have." She smiled at Stanley. "That okay with you?"

"An excellent selection," the waitress said insincerely, and left.

Ronnie raised her glass and tapped it against Stanley's. "To old lovers," she said. "And to cutting the crap. So," she took another sip, and when the glass left her lips her smile was gone. "I heard your company's being liquidated in bankruptcy. Shame."

"You did?" Stanley asked, surprised. "How?"

"In due time. You taking it okay?"

"My financial situation is, shall we say, awkward. Otherwise, no problem."

Ronnie set the glass gingerly on the table and traced a small circle beside it. "Yeah. I heard it cost you and Dave and Pete a bundle."

Stanley's eyes widened with astonishment. "Where?" blurted out. Many more bewildered questions churned in his mind, not the least of them being, *Do you know about Pete?*

But Ronnie waved away the inquiry. "Like I said. In due

time." She took another sip of wine, letting it linger on her tongue before swallowing it. "Didn't I tell you this was good? Now where was I. Oh yes. Getting wiped out by the bankruptcy. Though the way I hear the story, the creditors are pretty much paid off and you'll pocket whatever the auction nets. Pretty good so far?"

Stanley stared back, silent.

"I also heard about Dave," Ronnie continued.

"What about him?"

She tapped a red-tipped finger against the side of her head. "Alzheimer's."

"Ronnie . . ." Stanley began. He felt as if he had been the subject of a surveillance and Ronnie had a copy of the report. He thought, *I* am *being watched.*

"Pete," Ronnie said. "In answer to your question."

"Pete what?"

"Told me all of this. That's part of the reason I'm here. Pete's funeral."

"Then you know?"

"My God! Of course I know!"

"I'm confused. I never thought of you and Pete as close."

"Really, Stanny," Ronnie chastised. "I'll explain everything in due time. But back to Dave. How bad is he?"

Stanley shrugged. "Hard to say. I mean, it's not good. But that being said, he seems to function okay. Some days are better than others. They have him on some experimental stuff. Might be helping."

"Does he know he's got it?"

"Of course he knows," Stanley said. "He's not stupid." He could feel his arm begin to shake. He propped his elbows on the table and cupped his chin in his palms, a position that often ameliorated the tendency of the muscles to spasm.

"I heard you never settled down, got married, had children,"

Ronnie said. "Bachelorhood been good for you?"

"Maybe I'm gay," Stanley said.

Ronnie pursed her lips and wagged a finger at him. "Of all the things you may be, Stanny, I can definitely say that gay isn't one of them."

"Never married, true. Children?" Stanley attempted a lascivious shrug, a gesture hinting at myriad sexual escapades in a licentious youth, and having done so became immediately embarrassed at suggesting having fathered unacknowledged and unsupported children. But if Ronnie's feminist feathers were ruffled she showed no sign. "You?"

"Never married. No children. Involved with anyone?"

Unsure how to play that, Stanley said, "Now and then. You?"

Ronnie shook her head. "Not anymore. Tell me about the Parkinson's."

Stanley choked. He coughed. He clamped his hands down against the surface of the table. His face flushed. He regarded the disease as a shameful secret, and its discovery by others like their learning he was a registered sex offender. "Exactly what don't you know about me, Ronnie?"

"For one thing, how long you've had it."

"I was diagnosed about five years ago." Stanley glanced furtively at his left hand, knowing it was twitching with all the subtlety of a flashing neon sign reading *Look at me, I've got Parkinson's*. The meds' ability to hold the tremors at bay was conditional at best, and when Stanley was feeling stress or under the weather, they were pretty much useless. He reached for his wine glass for emotional support, a prop, something for his hand to do, and looked up at her. "Could you tell?"

"I can see your hand's shaking. Although I'm not sure I'd have noticed if I hadn't been told. If it's not being presumptuous to ask, what's it like?"

"You really want to know? Or just being polite?"

Ronnie patted his quivering hand. "Of course I want to know."

"Physically? My arm shakes intermittently. My handwriting's gone to hell. I can't manipulate things the way I used to. I get uncomfortable in crowds. I'm losing my sense of smell. Sometimes my head feels wobbly, like a mild case of seasickness. Sometimes it's hard to swallow. Sometimes I have trouble with certain words. Clothes resist me. Buttons refuse to go through holes. Sleeves corkscrew when I try to get my arms through. And then of course there's the anxiety and fatigue and other side effects of the medication. Not to mention that everything else that happens to me, like not being able to bench press as much as I used to, I always have to ask, is it the Parkinson's, or just the natural effects of aging, or something else entirely?" Stanley laughed sardonically. "It's a full-service disease. But mostly . . ." He tapped his fingers against the base of his wine glass. "Mostly, I feel like wherever I go, I'm the pink elephant in the room."

"Is there any good news? I hear about stem cell research."

"The only good news about Parkinson's is, it's a disease you die with, not from. Unfortunately, that's also the bad news."

"So it's not life threatening?"

"No," Stanley said. "Just quality of life threatening. Can we talk about something else?"

Ronnie reached into her purse and pulled out her pack of cigarettes. She looked at it, frowned and dropped it back in her purse. "Denial's not good, Stanny."

"Who says I'm in denial? I just don't want to talk about it."

"It's healthy to talk about problems." She shrugged. "But okay, let's change the subject. I heard you and Dave opened a detective agency. Can I tell you how impressed I am?"

"What's so impressive about that?" Stanley asked as the waitress appeared with two appetizers that she placed in the center of the table.

Ronnie grabbed a knife and fork and cut each appetizer in half. She put one of each on her bread plate and gestured to Stanley to eat from the service plates. She sliced off a small piece of wasabi-encrusted tuna and chewed it thoughtfully. "Respectable," she pronounced. "Not Napa, but respectable." She put her fork down. "Don't be so modest, Stanny. To start a new career. And to bring Dave along. With his condition."

"He's been my business partner for thirty years," Stanley said. "And my best friend for more."

"Even so." She switched to the crab cake, took a bite and grimaced. "Inedible." She scanned the restaurant furiously, as if searching for the cause of the atrocity. "I was told this was one of your best restaurants."

Stanley felt as if he were being personally attacked. He tried to deflect her anger with, "On behalf of the City of Chicago, I apologize."

Ronnie took a deep breath. "Sorry," she said. "I've been in an airplane all day. Throws off my metabolism. Damn! I need a cigarette."

"If you need to leave . . ." Stanley offered.

Ronnie waved away the suggestion. "I'll be okay. Where were we?"

"Lousy appetizers."

"Right." Ronnie set her fork down and clasped her hands together. "Which brings me to why I'm here."

"Lousy appetizers?"

"Private investigators. But to know why, you need to know what I do. I'm a connector."

"Connector?"

"I connect people with interesting ideas to people who want to invest in interesting ideas."

"You mean financial advisor? Venture capital?"

"More specialized. Hollywood's created all these idiosyncratic multimillionaires. Don't get me wrong, they read the P&Ls and do their homework, but the bottom line for them is, it's got to have sex appeal. Make a good story to tell at a cocktail party. That's who my clients are, and that's what they're looking for."

"A broker, then?"

"Only in the sense that I make the introductions and get a commission if it flies."

"I thought you went to Hollywood to become an actress."

"Oh, Stanny." Ronnie sighed. "Out of a thousand people who go to Hollywood to break into the movies, you know how many make it?" She held up her thumb and forefinger and made a circle. "Zero."

"So how did you get into the business you're in?"

A shadow passed across Ronnie's face. For a moment she seemed to be looking deep into the past, at forks in roads and choices made. "I was lucky."

"Glad to hear things worked out."

"Which brings me back to why I'm here. I'm working on a really sexy project. And I need your help." She paused and added, "Professional, I mean."

"I gather it involves contests and games?"

"No, no, no. I don't mean that. I mean, I need a detective."

Stanley laughed. He put down his fork. He looked at Ronnie and laughed again. "You're kidding. Right?"

"I'm serious, Stanny."

"Ronnie," Stanley said patiently, "please don't repeat this, but do you have any idea why Dave and I opened a detective agency? To get cheap health insurance. The only business we conduct is paying the premium every month." He immediately regretted the indiscretion. "I shouldn't have told you that," he said.

"Well, honestly, Stanny," she said. "I knew that."

Astonished, Stanley asked, "You did?"

"I already explained." She speared another piece of tuna. "Pete told me."

"Yeah. Pete. You know, I can't remember him ever mentioning talking to you."

Ronnie leaned back in her chair. She grabbed the stem of her wine glass and slowly spun it. "Well, Stanny, that was complicated. Pete and I . . . well, we were . . ."

Stanley didn't need her to complete the sentence. His left arm was beginning to quake harder. He quickly crossed his arms over his chest to calm the tremors. Even as she spoke the words, he saw the obviousness. It was exactly what Nick said. The thing Pete wouldn't talk about. The reason Pete kept him at arm's length. The explanation of the nagging sense that there were details Pete deliberately withheld. The reason, for that matter, that Pete never married.

But in one significant respect Nick was wrong. It was definitely personal.

"Why didn't he tell me?" Stanley asked.

"Out of sensitivity to you. He thought it would upset you to know." She looked disdainfully at the crab cake, then put her napkin on the table. "Look, you mind if I take you up on your offer to leave? I really need a cigarette."

"Fine with me," Stanley said. He had already lost his appetite.

Ronnie flagged the waitress for the check.

Stanley drank as much wine as he could while Ronnie's credit card was being processed, regretting he didn't have anything stronger.

CHAPTER 8

Outside, Ronnie jabbed a cigarette in her mouth, lit it and inhaled deeply. "That's better."

"Ever try to quit?" Stanley asked as he turned up the collar of his overcoat. Snow had started to fall while they were in the restaurant, and the sidewalk was dusted white.

"Of course I've tried," Ronnie said. "Problem is, I fly too much, and I get air sick. Can't do anything about it on the plane. But once I'm off, tobacco's the only thing that gets me past it. Besides, I'm too upset about Pete to quit now."

"I know what you mean," Stanley said.

"You have no idea what I mean," Ronnie replied curtly.

"Sorry," Stanley apologized. "I didn't mean to suggest that I could understand what it must be like for your lover to be murdered."

"Oh, that's so charmingly naive, Stanny," Ronnie said. "I didn't love Pete."

"But I thought you said . . ."

"I used to sleep with him." Ronnie snorted. "That's what I always find so precious about men, Stanny. You're such romantics. You think sex and love are inseparable. Pete was the same way. If you can believe it, there was a time he actually thought I was going to leave Hollywood and move to Chicago. Or let him move there and live with me. Took him years to come to terms with the fact that it wasn't about to happen." They turned north on Michigan Avenue. "No, what I'm upset

87

about is how he screwed me over."

Stanley stopped walking. "What did he do to you, Ronnie?"

"It's not what he did. It's what he didn't do. Which is why I need to hire you. As a detective."

"We back to that again?"

"Keep walking." Ronnie gave Stanley a gentle tug. "I think after I'm done explaining it, you'll understand that it's not only a job you can handle, but a job you're the best person to handle."

Stanley shrugged. "If you say so."

"But I have to ask you some questions first."

"Why?"

"In due time. Just think of it as a job interview. Okay?"

"I don't think I've ever been interviewed for a job," Stanley said.

"The upside and downside of working in a family business. Welcome to the real world." Ronnie took a deep last drag, flicked the cigarette onto the sidewalk, paused to light another, hooked her arm around Stanley's and resumed walking. "Tell me about Homebase," she said.

Stanley stopped abruptly. "Homebase?"

Ronnie sighed. "Can we please keep walking?" Smoke trickled from her mouth as she spoke. "Homebase. As in the Homebase Jamos Company bought for ten million dollars. Which, if my information is correct, Jamos Company didn't have and had to borrow to buy and couldn't pay back. As in the Homebase that drove Jamos Company into bankruptcy. That Homebase."

"Ronnie, what's this all about?"

"The project I told you I was working on? Homebase." She draped her hand on his arm. "In due time, Stanny. In due time. We've got a lot of ground to cover. Come on." She pulled at his arm. "Walk. Tell me about it."

"It's a website," Stanley said.

"For what?"

"For whom. Gen Y people who listen to alternative, indie, emo. Wait a minute," Stanley said, stopping again. "Why are you asking these questions? You obviously know all about it from Pete."

Ronnie exhaled smoke out of the side of her mouth to keep it from blowing into Stanley's face. "Job interview, remember? I need to hear about it from you. Will you please keep walking?"

"Need?" Stanley asked.

"Stanny, you sure do know how to blow a job interview. Look. I told you. In due time. Come on. It's too cold to stand still." She linked her arm around his and got him moving again.

"So what do you want to know?" Stanley asked.

"Why did you buy it?"

"To make Jamos Company more saleable."

"How so?"

"That's complicated," Stanley said. "We weren't ready to put the company on the market . . ."

"No, no," Ronnie interjected. "I know all about that. How was it supposed to make you more saleable?"

"By giving us a competitive edge nobody else had," Stanley said. "For which you need to understand what Homebase is from a marketing perspective. It's a tool to reach that demographic. The kids who listen to alternative music."

"To sell them what?"

"Whatever you want."

"What do they buy?"

Stanley shrugged. "Music. Clothes. Who knows?"

"So you'd, what? Sell ad space to record companies?"

"That was part of it. But it was so much more than that."

"Then give me an example."

"Fine. Here's a fairly generic idea. Let's say you make a product that Gen Y thinks of as past tense and you want to change its image. So you put together a series of hip pop-ups and launch them on Homebase. It's not necessarily to sell the product. Doesn't even have to be something that would ordinarily get marketed to that age group. You just want to plant the idea it's cool. So when they're ready to buy whatever it is you sell, they'll at least think of you, instead of writing you off. Bear in mind that this is an otherwise unreachable demographic. The kids who sign up on Homebase don't read newspapers. They get their information on the Internet."

"How did it make money?"

"Mostly sales of ad space." Stanley paused. "I think. At least that's how it was supposed to make money. Eventually," he added.

"In other words, it didn't make money."

"Not when we bought it," Stanley said. "Not when we went bankrupt, either," he admitted.

"How about now?"

For a moment Stanley felt suffocated by memories of the traumatic downfall of his company. "I can't say I've paid much attention. Pete ran it. I'd ask every now and then how it was doing. He said it was coming along."

"When was the last time you saw a financial statement?"

Stanley stopped walking again. "Ronnie, what's this about?"

"Stanny," Ronnie said, grabbing his hand again, "I know I'm being cryptic, but there's a reason." She tossed the cigarette on the sidewalk. It melted a small concrete circle into the white powdery snow until the water snuffed it out. "After your company tanked . . . that was thoughtless of me. After your company filed for bankruptcy, Pete called me and said I should put a group together to buy it. Homebase, I mean. He said it was worth a fortune, and nobody reading the auctioneer's bid package would get a clue as to its real value." She lit another cigarette.

"And did you? Put a group together?"

"That's why I'm talking to you," she said, staring in the window of a jewelry store.

The missing piece dawned on Stanley. He felt his hand starting to shake. "And what was in it for Pete?" he asked quietly.

"It would be his baby," Ronnie said nonchalantly. "He'd run it."

"CEO? That's all?"

"Of course not. He'd get a piece of the deal for packaging it."

"That bastard!"

Ronnie turned and looked at Stanley. She reached out, put her hand on Stanley's cheek and gently turned his head to face hers. "Stanny," she said. "It wasn't that way at all."

"Really?" Stanley said icily. "I mean, shame on me for not paying closer attention, but clearly he saw its potential and went to you to buy it out of the bankruptcy and in the process cut me out. And didn't even have the balls to tell me to my face. So you tell me. What way was it?"

"Hey!" Ronnie said. She dropped her hand to Stanley's arm and let it rest there. "He thought he was doing you a favor. After all, if the auction brought in more money, you made more money. From his perspective, what he was putting together was going to make you a lot more money than you'd have made otherwise. And to be perfectly honest, he didn't think you had the energy to stay involved in it. Which I have to tell you, Stanny. Seeing you tonight. He was wrong about that."

"You know," Stanley said, "I always had the sense that Pete was holding something back from me. So when you told me about your affair, I figured that's what it was. But now this. Makes me wonder what else he kept from me."

Ronnie cleared her throat. "Stanny? You done?"

"I'm livid!" Stanley snapped.

"Then be livid and walk. Okay? It's snowing. Come on. I'm trying to do us both a favor."

"And how's that?"

"Get my boys to pay a fortune for Homebase. The more they pay, the bigger my commission. And the bigger your take from the auction. Make lemons into lemonade," Ronnie said as they resumed walking.

After a moment's silence, Stanley asked, "That it?"

Ronnie nodded. "That was your job interview."

"Some interview. Seems to me you already knew the answers to all your questions."

Ronnie squeezed Stanley's hand. "Hardly. I knew Pete's answers. I didn't know yours. If your description of Homebase didn't match Pete's, that would be enough for my boys to walk."

"Oh," Stanley said. "Did I pass?"

"Flying colors."

"Hurray for me."

"Don't you want to know what you interviewed for?"

"I'm all ears."

Ronnie waved her cigarette, making circles in the air. "The problem wasn't putting together a group to buy Homebase. That was easy. The hard part was persuading them that it was worth what Pete said it was. So he was working on an analysis, all the data my group would need to become, shall we say, motivated buyers. Sales, prospects, projections . . ."

"Proprietary information, in other words."

"If you want to put it that way."

"He had no right to do that," Stanley said, bristling. "That information belonged to the company."

"And the company belongs to its creditors, and all they care about is maximizing the bids at the auction," Ronnie countered. "I mean, come off it, Stanny. This isn't corporate espionage or insider trading or anything even remotely close. But that's neither here nor there. Before he could deliver it, what does the idiot do? Goes and gets himself killed. And for what? Walks in on a robbery. Probably could have called nine-one-one, but wanted to be the tough guy."

"How do you know?" Stanley asked. "You weren't there to see what really happened."

"I know how his mind worked," Ronnie said bitterly. She looked up at Stanley. "But that's the problem, Stanny. He never got me the analysis." She scowled and flicked her cigarette into a garbage can. "Leaving me in the lurch."

"Well, I hope you're not expecting me to pinch hit for him," Stanley said. "It was Pete's project, start to finish. I never knew that much about it."

"Stanny, if I thought you could tell my boys what they need to know, this would be a much different proposition. No, Pete made it perfectly clear he was the only one in your company with in-depth knowledge of how Homebase worked. What I need you to do is find the analysis he was writing."

"And where am I supposed to look?"

"Isn't it obvious? Your office."

"Ronnie," Stanley said patiently, "the office is closed. We rejected the lease in the bankruptcy."

"Not the downtown office. The other office. Where Pete worked. In the suburbs."

"The warehouse? Bensenville?" Stanley said. "What makes you think it would be there?"

"He told me that's where he was working on it. Where the files were. Makes sense, doesn't it?"

"Oh," Stanley said uncertainly. Then he realized where Ronnie was leading him. "You need me to get you in the warehouse so you can look for it."

"Would that I had the time," Ronnie sighed. "I'm juggling too many balls as it is. No, I was serious when I said I needed your detective services. I'd like to hire you to find it." She paused to stare at a store window display of shoes and handbags.

"Why me? Don't you want a real detective?"

"Because you can get in there. Legally, I mean. Who else can I hire who can do that? And you also know where things are inside. See what I mean? If there ever was a job designed specifically for you, this is it."

"But what am I looking for? A computer file? There's probably twenty laptops and a mainframe there. You'd need an army of geeks."

"Stanny," Ronnie interrupted. "I've seen it. To the extent he'd finished it the last time he flew out to L.A. Written on yellow legal pads."

The thought of Pete having a Los Angeles liaison with Ronnie left an empty feeling in Stanley's gut. "What if it isn't there? Or it is, but hidden where I can't find it?"

"I'll cross that bridge when I come to it," Ronnie said. "Meanwhile, let's at least look for it." She turned to face Stanley. Her tongue darted across her lips. Her eyes were imploring, not lascivious, but the tongue stirred memories of her mouth's adept talents.

"You can do this," she said.

After a pause, Stanley asked, "Yellow legal pads?"

Ronnie nodded as she opened her purse, reached in and pulled out a paper that she handed to Stanley.

Stanley looked at it in the light of a store window. A check drawn on an R. DUMAT account for five thousand dollars. Issued to the order of JAMOS AND MOSIT DETECTIVES.

She asked, "That seem reasonable?"

Stanley stared at the check. He looked down at Ronnie. He folded the check and slipped it into his overcoat pocket. "You just hired yourself a detective," he said.

Ronnie stood up on the tips of her shoes and kissed Stanley softly on the lips. "You won't regret it."

"I can't guarantee anything."

Ronnie shrugged. "I have faith in you, Stanny." She winked. "No guarantees."

★ ★ ★ ★ ★

TUESDAY

★ ★ ★ ★ ★

CHAPTER 9

The diner was eerily quiet. Stanley held the door open, replaying "Jingle Bells" in case Tracy had missed it the first time. Still no Tracy. He closed the door, grabbed a *Tribune* from the stack, removed the sports section and carried it to a table and spread it open. He tried to get interested in the predictions about how the Cubs and White Sox would fare in the coming season, but his mind kept drifting back to Ronnie, how she had looked, the job for which she had hired him. His knees kept bouncing. He couldn't keep still. He refolded the section, got up, grabbed the rest of the paper and a cup of decaf and brought them back to the table.

He was reading about a road rage episode on the Dan Ryan Expressway that had left three people hospitalized when the swinging kitchen doors banged. Tracy stomped out and sat at the stool behind the register. Stanley smiled at her. She avoided looking at him. Stanley resumed reading the paper. A moment later he heard the ring of the cash box opening. He looked up. Tracy smashed a roll of quarters into the register and slammed it shut. She looked angry. He nodded at her. She didn't acknowledge him.

He called, "Hey, Tracy!"

She looked away.

Stanley folded the paper, got up and walked over to the register. As he got closer to Tracy he saw the tear-streaked mascara and the cover-up troweled over the left eye, which was swollen and, he suspected, black and blue underneath. "Tracy!" he exclaimed. "Is everything alright?"

Tracy began to sniffle.

Stanley pushed the metal napkin dispenser on the counter toward her. "What's wrong?" he asked.

Tears began pooling in her eyes. "Jake walked out on me last night."

Stanley said, "Tracy, I'm so sorry."

"He's seeing someone else. Says my buying this place drove him to it." Her shoulders began to quake. She looked at Stanley through earnest, watery eyes. "Now all of a sudden it was all my doing. He says I have to buy him out. Or else sell the place and give him half the money." Tears began to trickle down her cheeks. "And it was my money we bought it with too, damn it. My inheritance. He didn't put up a single penny. It was all I had." She yanked a wad of napkins from the dispenser and dabbed at her eyes. "Can he make me do that?"

"I'm no lawyer," Stanley said. "Tracy?"

Tracy turned away, as if doing so would hide the fact of her crying.

"Tracy?" Stanley repeated softly. When she turned to face him he asked gently, "Did he hit you?"

Between sobs, she nodded.

"Did you call the police?"

She shook her head, dropped the crumpled napkins onto the counter, grabbed more, wiped her eyes and tossed them on top of the others. "I don't even know where he is."

"You have to call the police and file a report," Stanley said. "Then call a divorce lawyer and find out what you should do. Change the locks on your doors. And don't go home tonight. Is there anyone you can stay with?"

Tracy bit her lip. She nodded her head.

"Then stay there."

Tracy made a valiant and failed effort to force a smile.

"I'm worried about you. You think you'll be safe here? Maybe you should close up. What if he comes around?"

"I'll be okay," she said. "Mike—the part-time cook. Guess he'll be promoted to full time now—he's here. And Raul, the dishwasher, ought to be showing up any time."

"Okay," Stanley said. "But the minute Jake walks in the door, you'll call nine-one-one?"

Tracy nodded, blinking away the tears. She started to rise, then flopped back down on the stool. "I don't know any divorce lawyers. You know any?"

"I think that's the only kind I never needed," Stanley said. "But I'll keep my ears open."

"And cheap," Tracy added. She looked around the diner. "Shit! When it all goes to hell, it sure goes in a hand basket, doesn't it?"

"That's not the half of it," Stanley agreed.

"Guess I'm not going to Honduras."

"You're young. Things change," Stanley said.

Stanley turned at the sound of "Jingle Bells." Dave and Cindy entered.

"Is my cover-up holding?" Tracy whispered frantically.

"You look great," Stanley said.

Tracy nodded at Dave and Cindy and said, "Morning. Coffee?"

Dave grinned at Tracy, walked to the table where Stanley had spread the *Tribune*, removed his overcoat and fedora and put them on the table. Cindy rolled her eyes, walked over to the table, picked up the coat and hat and hung them on the peg. When she returned to Stanley and Tracy by the register she saw the heap of tear-soaked napkins. Then she looked at Tracy and frowned. "You okay, dear?" she asked.

"I'm fine, thanks," Tracy said. She swept the napkins off the counter and into the garbage can by the register. "The usual?" she asked Stanley.

"Pancakes for both of us," Stanley said. "I think I'm done with eggs for a while."

"You having breakfast too?" Tracy asked Cindy.

Cindy glanced at her watch and shook her head. "I'm running late as it is."

"Can you wait a second, Cindy?" Stanley asked. "Come over here." He led her back to the table. "I got news." He clasped Dave on the shoulder. "I met with our first client last night."

Cindy looked uncomprehending for a moment, then incredulous. "Detective client?"

Stanley nodded.

The words, "Someone actually hired you?" blurted out of Cindy's mouth. Her face turned crimson. "I didn't mean it that way," she hastily apologized, but she couldn't stop her eyes from telegraphing, *Who in his right mind would do that?*

Stanley answered her unspoken question. "An old college friend. Turns out she put together a group that's bidding on one of the company's assets. Wants me to help her get a leg up on the competition." He deliberately avoided mention of Pete's involvement.

"A real job? As in getting paid?"

"Five thousand," Stanley said.

"Wow." Cindy crooked a finger at Stanley, signaling him to follow her several feet away from her husband. "Look," she whispered, "you need me to take Dave off your hands?"

"Not at all," Stanley said. He reached in his jacket pocket and pulled out the check and showed it to her. "That's Jamos and Mosit. The two of us. Detectives." He grinned.

"If you're sure," Cindy said. She returned to the table, bent over Dave, kissed him on his bald spot and said, "See you for dinner." Hovering over her husband's head, she looked up at

Stanley. "You'll let me know? If you need to work by yourself?"

"We'll be fine," Stanley said. "Enjoy the day."

Staring at the top of Dave's head, her fingers parting his hair, she said softly, "I worry about you."

"Don't worry about Dave. He'll be fine," Stanley said.

"I meant you," she said. She turned away and left the diner without looking back at Dave or Stanley.

Stanley sat as Tracy brought their breakfasts on a tray, pancakes for Dave and eggs sunny side up for Stanley, orange juice for both.

Stanley stared at the eggs, perplexed. "Didn't I . . . ?" he began.

"Something wrong?" Tracy asked, looking on the verge of another crying jag.

"Nothing," Stanley said.

When Tracy left he pushed the fork to Dave's side of the table, as if to get rid of its mocking presence. He spooned egg in inelegant globs onto a piece of whole wheat toast, took a bite, chewed, tossed in the morning's dose of meds and washed it all down with orange juice.

They ate in silence, Dave staring the whole time at a photograph of a promising White Sox rookie pitcher. When Stanley finished his breakfast he dipped a napkin into his water glass, wiped his fingers and said, "Yesterday I asked if you remembered Ronnie Dumat."

"Who?"

"My girlfriend from college. Senior year. You said a picture might help. So I brought this." Stanley reached into his inner jacket pocket and pulled out a photograph. He gazed at it wistfully, at the young woman in the miniskirt and halter top and long black ironed hair, eyes owlish with mascara, leaning against a tree, smiling, holding a cigarette. Then he passed it to Dave. "Recognize her?"

Dave nodded. "Ronnie Dumat."

"She came to see me yesterday. Hired us, Dave."

Dave looked uncertain. "Hired us?"

"You want to hear what the job is?"

"Job?"

"Search the warehouse. That's where we're headed after breakfast." He added, "I tell you, Dave, I got a good feeling about this."

Dave asked cautiously, "The Jamos Company warehouse?"

"Right."

"Do we still work there?"

"We do today," Stanley said

"Jingle Bells" played. Over Dave's shoulder he saw Doug and Tim enter the diner. Tim waved. Doug called out, "Well, well," walked over to the table, Tim in tow, and asked, "Mind if we join you?" He glanced at Ronnie's picture as he sat, then looked at Stanley. "Let me guess. Missing person?"

"Not anymore," Stanley said. He tried to pick up the photograph, but his fingertips floundered for traction. The effort was too frustrating. He gave up and left the picture on the table.

Tim dropped his duffel bag on the floor and pulled out a chair. Tracy stopped by with her two coffeepots and poured regular all around despite Stanley's effort to block her from filling his cup.

Doug and Tim each ordered the *Chef Recommends*, Tim's with a side of hash browns. "Great suggestion," Tim told Stanley after Tracy left to place the orders. "Dad was in a good mood all day yesterday. And believe you me, I don't see too many of those."

"You'd think it would taste like shit, but it's really good," Doug added. He emptied a creamer in his coffee and downed the whole cup.

"So what kinds of cases do you take?" Tim asked. "Besides missing persons?"

"Cases?" Dave asked.

"Let me guess," Doug said. "A little this, a little that. But mostly wives wanting proof their hubby's banging someone else." His booming voice filled the room as he carried his cup to the warmer for a refill. "I bet they come on all boo-hoo how they hope it ain't true, but what they really want is good photos to extort more in the divorce." He winked at Tracy, seated behind the register. "Am I right or am I right?"

"Sure," she said listlessly.

"What's her beef?" Doug asked as he returned to the table.

"She just found out her husband's having an affair," Stanley said quietly. "He walked out on her last night. Leaving her short a husband and a cook."

"Looks like he roughed her up a little, too," Tim said. His tone was so indifferent, so devoid of anger, compassion, concern, any emotion, that Stanley surmised in Tim's world such events were commonplace.

"I'm a little worried about her being here on her own," Stanley added.

"That kind of stuff mostly happens at night when the guy's had a few too many," Tim observed. He held up his hand, palm forward. "Not saying it's okay, just that it ain't that likely he'll show up here. But me and Dad'll come check every once in a while. Won't we, dad?"

"I was making a point," Doug said. "Don't none of you care?"

"Dad," Tim said, "did you hear anything we just said?"

"Sure. Check up on her. You think I'm deaf? But what I was getting at . . . aw, crap. You made me forget."

"Sorry," Tim said with transparent insincerity.

"Hey!" Doug said. "If her husband was the cook, who's making my breakfast?"

"Dad, her husband's a wife beater," Tim said.

"I ain't nominating him for the Nobel Peace Prize. I just want my breakfast. If it's all the same with you." Doug picked up the picture of Ronnie. "Nice-looking babe."

"Ronnie Dumat," Dave said.

Doug put the picture back on the envelope. "Why'd she run away?"

"Drugs, probably," Tim speculated. "Or an uncle getting too friendly."

The swinging kitchen doors banged and a pair of arms passed a tray through. Tracy got up, took it, brought it to the table and set plates before Doug and Tim.

"I remember the point I was making," Doug said, slicing his *Chef Recommends* into bite-sized pieces. "My point was, if I was in the detective business, I wouldn't believe a word my clients told me. Because things are never what they seem."

"You watch too many movies, Dad," Tim said. "Hell, nothing's ever what it seems. Besides, you don't trust nobody anyway."

"Sound advice," Doug said. He looked at Stanley. "Don't trust nobody. You'll thank me for that some day."

"Speaking of things not being what they seem," Tim said, smacking the bottom of the catsup bottle and smothering his hash browns, "I was thinking about you two. Nobody would ever figure you for detectives. And then," snapping his fingers, "I got it. That's what makes you good at it. Being in . . . in . . . not standing out like sore thumbs."

"Inconspicuous," Stanley offered.

"What I said," Tim said through a mouthful of potatoes.

"Although that's hardly how I'd describe us."

"Whatever." Tim jabbed his fork in Stanley's direction. "What do you guys charge?"

A question Stanley had never anticipated. He quickly tried to recall every detective movie he'd seen and book he'd read. The answer was always some daily rate plus expenses but he had no idea what was appropriate. "Depends," he said, hoping he sounded more nonchalant than evasive.

"Depends on what?"

To which, Stanley realized with astonishment, he had a real-world answer: "The assignment. For example, the one we're on now is five thousand."

Tim and Doug exchanged eyebrow-arched glances. "For a missing person?" Tim said. "Sounds like a lot of green."

"Not to me," Doug said. "Not for a missing kid. Not if it were mine, anyway."

"You'd drop five grand to find me, dad?"

"Who said anything about finding you? I'm talking about making sure you stay missing." He turned to Dave and slapped him on the shoulder and laughed, spraying small flecks of *Chef Recommends* onto Dave's plate.

"A word of advice," Tim said, stuffing the last of the hash browns in his mouth and slicing up the *Chef Recommends*. "Never work with your father."

"Too late," Stanley said.

"Because necrotism never works."

"Nepotism?"

"What I said." Tim jabbed his fork at Stanley. "Mind if I ask you a professional question?"

Stanley shrugged. "Go ahead."

"Guy comes in the other day with some necklaces and rings. Got some pretty hefty stones. I figure they'll bring in fifty grand easy. But here's his problem. He needs to get his babe a watch. Gold. Right away. And he can't front the money himself."

"So he says," Doug interjected.

"Offers we pop for the watch, sell the goods, take out our expenses and split the net. Dad and me figure we can get the watch for twenty grand, which means fifteen profit after the split. That's a real nice chunk of change. Return on investment, as Dad would put it. So we say okay."

"So you said okay," Doug grumbled. "I wasn't there."

Tim bristled. "So I said okay."

"So you got greedy."

"Whatever." Tim was now waving his fork like an agitated orchestra conductor. "The point, which you probably already figured out, is the goods were hot, the guy's name and address are made up and the phone number he gave us don't exist."

"That's what you get for being greedy," Doug said, shaking his head.

"So you made your point earlier, Dad. Don't trust nobody. What do you want me to do about it?"

"Find the asshole," Doug said. "Break his kneecaps."

Tim speared his last piece of the special. "You think you can find the asshole?" he asked Stanley.

"Not if you expect me to break his kneecaps," Stanley said.

"But can you find . . ."

"Come on, what do you think he's going to tell you?" Doug said. "He's a PI. Of course he's going to tell you he can find the guy." He tossed his fork onto his plate.

Tim glared at Doug. "You mind if I ask anyway?" He turned back to Stanley. "You think you can do it?"

"Well . . ." Stanley said.

"You're interrupting the man's breakfast," Doug said. "He's going to ask you to make an appointment and sign a retainer agreement and all that crap."

"Sorry," Tim said. "I don't mean to be rude talking business over breakfast. Can we stop by your office sometime and discuss this?"

"Well . . ." Stanley said.

"Not if we're talking five grand we ain't," Doug said. He

belched into his fist, turned and flagged Tracy.

Tim leaned close to Stanley and asked quietly, "Can we talk a minute? Somewhere else?" He rose and backed away from the table.

Stanley nodded. "Sure." He excused himself to Dave, got up and followed Tim to the far end of the diner.

"Here's the deal," Tim said. "You strike me as a sharp guy. But the reason Dad's being such a jerk is he's worried about your partner. That he'll mess things up. I had a hard time selling you because of that. You know what I mean?"

"Look, I won't be insulted if you use someone else."

Tim clapped Stanley on the shoulder. "What I told you the other day. You're a saint, man. For taking care of your friend. It's the least I can do. You got a card?"

"Card," Stanley said. He made a point of patting at his jacket pocket, then shrugged. "Sorry. Don't seem to have any on me."

"Never mind. I know where your office is."

Stanley heard Doug exclaim, "You shitting me?" from behind. He turned. Dave was holding the photograph of Ronnie, showing it to Doug, grinning. Doug looked ready to take a swing at someone.

Stanley moved quickly to the table. "Something wrong?"

"I'll say there is," Doug said, scowling. "Your friend here claims to have slept with the missing person."

"That's impossible," Stanley said.

Dave turned the picture to Stanley. "Yes, I did," he said, his head bobbing up and down with childlike pride, like he was showing off a new bike. "She was great!"

Stanley felt as though he'd slammed into a wall of bricks. His chest constricted. His heart throbbed. He panicked that he might pass out. The fraction of a second it took for Dave to add, "She was great," seemed interminable. He reached for a chair back for support, fighting to resist the tremors he knew were imminent.

Dave was looking at Stanley expectantly for an encouraging response. Stanley reached out and yanked the photograph from Dave's hand and stuffed it back in his jacket pocket. "You have to excuse him," he muttered. "It's the . . ."

"Yeah, I understand," Tim said. "Come on, Dad. Let's go."

Stanley felt on the verge of vomiting breakfast. Bile was rising, and a foul taste had crept into the back of his mouth. He tossed a twenty and a ten on the table, too much, but his only concern was fresh air. "Let's get out of here," he muttered. He passed Doug at the register, brusquely nodded goodbye to Tracy, and exited carrying his overcoat, not looking back to confirm that Dave was following. His need for fresh air had become desperate.

Outside he took a deep breath. The morning hinted of spring. A gentle breeze blew from the south, and the sun was bright in the cloudless sky. His hand began to shake. He was amazed it had stayed still so long. He put his overcoat on the roof of the car, got the key from his pants pocket and beeped the doors unlocked. He looked at the hand holding the key. It seemed unconnected to him, as if he was watching it in a movie. He opened the rear door and tossed the overcoat on the back seat. He watched Dave open the front door, passenger side, and crawl in. Dave seemed to move in slow motion. In the periphery of his vision he saw Doug and Tim exit the diner. He could hear them talking about a game they'd watched the night before. He turned to face them. Tim pointed a finger at him, as if he was firing a gun, and winked. Stanley nodded, frightened by the gesture. Everything seemed warped and ominous.

Stanley opened the driver's side door, paused and reconsidered. Once the ignition started his telephone would transmit through the car radio speakers. He wanted to make a call and he wanted it to be private. "Just a second," he told Dave. He shut the door and called Cindy.

"Tell me about Dave's memory," he said.

"What do you mean?"

"How much he's got. How good it is."

"Well, you ought to spend enough time with him to know," Cindy said. "His short-term memory is shot. Although he seems better since they put him on that new protocol."

"It's not his short-term memory I'm interested in."

"Long term? That's funny. No, not funny. Amazing at times. He remembers stuff I completely forgot. Stuff I would have assumed he'd forgotten. Stuff he should have forgotten. Dumb things I did thirty years ago. You want to really see something? Show him an old photograph. If it's one of him or one he took, he can give you details about what's going on like he's right there. It's kind of weird."

"How reliable is it? What he remembers? Long term, I mean?" Stanley's anxiety was palpable. He feared Cindy heard the high-pitched nervous quaver in his voice.

"Like I said. He comes up with stuff I forgot. Come to think of it," she added, "the doctor talked to me about that. Said to expect his long-term memory to be surprisingly good even as everything else goes. Why do you ask?"

"But if you forgot, how do you know it's accurate? I mean, when he remembers things from way back? How can you tell what's real and what's he's making up?"

"Why would he make stuff up?" Cindy asked.

"Dave was telling me some things he did in college," Stanley said. "Some of it was dead on. But some of it seemed too implausible to be real. But he believed all of it. So I just wondered. Whether when he remembers things, if any of it is made up."

"Not like Dave to make stuff up. He was never the imaginative type before he got sick. You know what I mean? But who knows? Maybe his meds are messing with his memory, what he's got left of it anyway. So what did he tell you?"

"Excuse me, that's an incoming call," Stanley lied. "I'll have to get back to you."

Stanley slid in the driver's seat. Dave was staring forward, a mischievous smile illuminating his face. His hat had fallen on the floor and was in danger of being stepped on. Stanley reached over, picked it up and placed it on the console between them before starting the car. Dave retrieved it and put it on his head. As Stanley started the engine Dave asked, "Where we going?"

"Jamos Company," Stanley said. "Back to work."

"We still work there?" Dave asked.

"Today we do," Stanley said. He put on his seat belt and adjusted his rearview mirror. An object reflected in it, halfway down the block, was out of place. A dark car. Big, four door. Too shiny to belong to any of the regulars. Hard to tell the make, but definitely American. That ruled out the developers who occasionally prowled the neighborhood. He felt a chill. *That's a police car,* he thought. *I* am *being watched.*

CHAPTER 10

A year after Stanley, Dave and Pete joined the company, Stanley's father had announced they were relocating to Bensenville.

Stanley was dismayed.

Since his childhood, the business had operated out of a converted factory building on South Michigan Avenue. The neighbors were rhythm and blues recording studios, Southern Baptist churches, soul food restaurants, hookers and junkies. It was quintessential Chicago. Stanley had loved it.

Stanley knew intuitively Bensenville was the wrong call. If the company had to relocate, it should be to some place with sizzle. But he had had no vote, and his father's case was compelling. Bensenville was next to O'Hare. Clients came to Chicago only to inspect the Jamos Company facility and had no desire to be far from the airport. Land was cheap.

They bought a warehouse. For the next eight years, Jamos Company made its presentations in a windowless conference room, and usually in Chicago's dreary winter. Sales remained flat.

At the first executive meeting after Stanley and Dave and Pete were made partners, Stanley floated moving to the Loop. He described the city's changing demographics, the Loop's amenities, his perception of the clients' personalities, and outlined a marketing and business development strategy.

Stanley's father's objection was predictable. He was at a different point on the career trajectory and comfortable with Bensenville. He tried to squelch further discussion with comments like, "I can see the time will come," to which Stanley heard an unstated *But not in my lifetime.* In this Stanley was almost prescient, since his father was experiencing an unfamiliar weariness, a symptom of his as-yet-undiagnosed inoperable cancer.

Stanley was counting on Dave. With the birth of their child, Dave and Cindy had moved from Old Town to an elite northern suburb. Dave had joined a country club and hobnobbed with executives who commuted to Loop offices. Stanley had told Dave about the idea in advance, expecting Dave to back it up with an economic justification. But Dave saw the issue strictly in terms of cost of assets and sided with Stanley's father.

Stanley hadn't expected support from Pete, whose energies in the intervening years had been devoted to computerizing the warehouse and designing security software. He was caught off guard when Pete declared that Stanley was right. His operations, he said, the nuts and bolts of the business, were fine in Bensenville, but the executive headquarters, marketing and sales, belonged in the Loop.

Stanley's father thought the compromise brilliant.

Stanley accepted his victory by biting his tongue. His father thought everything Pete said and did was brilliant.

Stanley rented a suite on an upper floor of a skyscraper on North Michigan Avenue, with acrophobia-inducing views of Lake Michigan and northbound Lake Shore Drive. He rescheduled client meetings and presentations to the summer. He bought a high-powered telescope for the conference room. He would wait ten or twenty minutes after the clients were shown in so the men could use it to check out the women sunbathing on the decks of the boats. Then he'd enter and begin his presentation by describing the safari to Rush Street for drinks and food that awaited them when it was over.

Presentations didn't take long.

Business spiked.

Stanley proved his point. He knew how to market.

After the move, Stanley's trips to the warehouse became so infrequent that there were times he drove right past it, the building too similar to the other yellow brick boxes on the industrial drive, the concrete monument sign with the Jamos Company name and logo too small and drab to command attention.

This time Stanley needn't have been concerned about recognizing the building. The auctioneer's sign, which Stanley hadn't seen before, stood out like yellow urine on freshly fallen snow. Huge block letters screamed BANKRUPTCY and FORCED LIQUIDATION and BY COURT ORDER.

He idled the car before pulling into the driveway and stared at the sign. It stared back, like a bully who punched him in the face and stood over him, sneering, defying him to stand up. It was the ultimate humiliation. Jamos Company, once the epitome of marketing sophistication, was being hawked like hot dogs at a baseball game.

Stanley had had his issues with his father, but he would never have wished for him to see this blasphemy, much less to attend the auction less than two months away. He knew exactly how his father would have reacted.

As the furniture and equipment went for a fraction of what they'd paid for it, enough, if they were lucky, to cover the legal expense of the bankruptcy, he'd turn away, his jaw muscles grinding, chain-smoking his mentholated cigarettes.

When the building went, even if it brought in the predicted million five, enough, after commission and expenses and the final payment to the bank, to repay most of Stanley's loans to the company, he'd be breathing in short, angry snorts.

But when he'd read the brochure on what was coming next,

some dumb-ass website they'd borrowed ten million to buy, the dam would break. *Homebase?* he would have exploded, making no effort to mask his anger, struggling only, if at all, with the urge to strike his son. And then, head shaking with rage, he'd fire off, *What in hell were you thinking? Ten million for that piece of shit?*

To which Stanley would have had no answer. He had bought Homebase, and in so doing destroyed what his father had built.

The auction would be Jamos Company's funeral. With the last bang of the gavel, Jamos Company would be pronounced dead and Stanley would walk away from the work of two lifetimes with some money in his pocket, a humiliating sense of personal failure, one friend dead, and one who might as well be.

The overcast sky and leafless trees sucked the life out of the warehouse, making it look like a mausoleum in a cemetery. As he pulled in the driveway he glanced at Dave to see if he had any reaction. But Dave was asleep. Not that Stanley would have expected much, even discounting the Alzheimer's. Dave in his good days would have assessed the sight with accountant's eyes, book value versus market value, or depreciable capital improvements versus deductible expenses. What Stanley longed for was Pete's reaction. The warehouse had been Pete's baby, and Stanley couldn't help but think that if Pete were here now, reading the auctioneer's sign on this dismal day, he'd be close to tears.

And then Stanley remembered that Pete had seen the sign. He'd seen it every time he drove to the warehouse to work on his project with Ronnie. And Stanley also remembered that while he had been cooped up in his office-that-wasn't-an-office, babysitting his partner-who-wasn't-a-partner, Pete had been commuting to Los Angeles, meeting with Ronnie's investors and going back to her place for wine and cheese and sex.

Stanley switched off the ignition. He looked at Dave, trying to make sense of Dave's stunning proclamation that morning about Ronnie. He stared into space, reflecting on how, in less than twenty-four hours, he'd learned that his two partners, two of his closest friends, had slept with the only woman he'd ever loved.

He felt wholly betrayed.

He couldn't shake the accompanying anxiety, the feeling that things weren't right, that something awful was about to happen. And once again the sense that he was being watched tingled like a centipede crawling up his spine.

I'm here on business, he reminded himself. He nudged Dave awake and said, "Let's go."

"To work?" Dave asked.

"To work."

Stanley swung his legs out of the car, pulled himself up using the roof for leverage, began to step away and found his foot stuck. He pitched forward. In a panic he grabbed at the door to prevent himself from falling, then panicked again that the momentum of his body would cause the door to slam on his hand.

His feet resisted his efforts to make them move. It felt as though he was trapped in tar. His neurologist had told him this sort of thing was unpredictable and ought not last longer than a few seconds. True; the muscles suddenly unfroze and he stepped away from the car.

"Come on," he muttered at Dave as if Dave were the one holding them up.

Stanley unlocked the door to the small reception room. It looked the same as it had when Jamos Company had been in business, save for the absence of the rotund, perpetually cheerful receptionist who sat behind the glass window doing her nails, greeting guests and answering the switchboard. The desk was as cluttered as if she was on one of her all-too-frequent cigarette breaks. He made a mental note to lodge a complaint with the trustee, but personally found the mess reassuring, a greeting from the past, a reminder of what Jamos Company had once been.

He opened the interior door and flipped on the light switches. The banks of suspended fluorescent lights flickered on in the cavernous room, humming in monotone and illuminating what was left of Jamos Company. Cartons of business records and files were stacked against one wall. Desks and file cabinets separated by black, tan and olive piled with computers, keyboards, monitors and printers covered another. The floor was barely navigable, littered with lamps, chairs and cardboard boxes.

Pete's oak roll-top desk was off to the side, an antique interloper at a gathering of contemporary.

Stanley pointed to the desk and told Dave, "There's the logical place to start."

"Start what, Stanley?" Dave asked.

"We're looking for an analysis of Homebase." Realizing that wouldn't have much meaning to Dave, he amended that to, "Some notes Pete made. My guess? They're either in his desk or the verification room." He walked over to the desk and tried to lift the top.

It was locked.

Stanley rummaged through the boxes on the floor until he found a screwdriver and hammer. He wedged the screwdriver into the desk lock and tapped it with the hammer until the lock opened. He set the tools on the floor and rolled back the top.

The cubbyholes were empty. The desk's bare surface was wiped clean. He opened the drawers and found nothing except a rubber band and a few paper clips. He rolled the top down and sighed. "I guess that would have been too easy. Let's try the verification room."

Stanley punched the access code in the numeric lock. The solenoid clicked. Stanley turned the doorknob. The door wouldn't budge.

Stanley thought, *Is it possible I just locked it?*

He re-entered the code. The solenoid clicked. He turned the knob. The door swung open.

Not like Pete to leave this room unlocked, Stanley thought as he stepped inside.

Pete's equipment was still in place, cameras and computers and backup systems. Stanley looked around while Dave stood by idly, swaying slightly. A yellow legal pad would have been conspicuous. The room lacked nooks and crannies.

"Oh, well," Stanley sighed. He shut the door, careful to re-enter the access code and lock it. He stretched and surveyed the desks and file cabinets and concluded, "Sure hope it's not in one of those. Come on, Dave. Let's take a look around."

Dave in tow, Stanley began with the offices. All the doors were wide open. There was nothing to search. Each room had been stripped, completely. Even the tattered, coffee-stained carpeting had been removed, probably at the direction of the auctioneer.

With diminishing optimism, Stanley searched the kitchen and bathrooms, the HVAC room and the electric closet. He found nothing. He returned to the warehouse and stared at the desks and file cabinets and crated office supplies with dismay and said, "What have I gotten myself in for?"

He looked at the door to the verification room.

"Pete wouldn't have left it open," he said.

He unlocked the door and entered and looked around again.

"I don't know, Dave," he said.

"Know what?"

"Know where he hid it." His gaze turned upward, to the

dropped ceiling. One acoustic tile was slightly out of alignment with the grid. "Well, look at that. Make a good hiding place, don't you think? Stay here." Stanley left and returned with a desk lamp and a chair. He plugged in the lamp, stood on the chair, pushed the tile up, and poked the lamp and his head through the opening.

"Well, that was a waste of time," he said. He replaced the tile, unplugged the lamp and shut and re-locked the door.

He looked again at the desks and file cabinets. He glanced at his watch. "Almost twelve," he told Dave.

"Midnight?" Dave asked. "Time for bed?"

Stanley looked up at the sunlight streaming in through the windows. He looked at Dave and thought, *This can't be a good sign.* Grabbing his overcoat, he said, "Noon, Dave. Time for lunch."

CHAPTER 11

It was a thirty-five-minute drive back to the diner, but Stanley wanted to check in on Tracy.

"You doing okay?" he asked her.

She sniffled and nodded. "Except I'm short-staffed. Raul never showed up."

Stanley looked around. The diner was empty. "So close early."

"What?" Tracy asked bitterly. "And disappoint all these customers?"

"Jake ever come by?"

Tracy shook her head.

"You report him to the police?"

"Yeah. And speaking of police. Those two officers you had lunch with the other day? They were here earlier, looking for you."

"My lucky day," Stanley muttered.

After ordering, Stanley and Dave sat in silence. Stanley flipped with disinterest through the pages of an out of date magazine. When Tracy brought their orders Stanley closed the magazine, pushed it aside and looked up at Dave.

Dave looked perplexed.

"Something wrong, Dave?" Stanley asked as Tracy placed a cheeseburger and a mound of fries glistening with grease before Dave and a three-decker bacon, lettuce and tomato on whole wheat before Stanley.

"Did something bad happen to Pete?"

121

"As bad as it gets, Dave. He was murdered."

"That's terrible." Dave's expression metamorphosed from confused to pensive. "Why didn't he have insurance?"

"Well, he might have. But what's the difference? It's not like he had a family to support."

Dave poured a small hill of catsup on his plate, dipped the cheeseburger in and took a bite. "Did I know he was murdered?"

Stanley chewed his lip. "Yes, Dave. You did."

"I forget, you know."

"I know," Stanley said.

"I have Alzheimer's," Dave explained.

"I know, Dave."

"I didn't remember if I told you." He nibbled on a fry. "I ought to know that Pete's dead. Shouldn't I?"

"It was pretty recent, Dave. It only happened a few days ago."

Dave picked up his cheeseburger and opened his mouth to take a bite, then put it back down on the plate. "What if something happened to Cindy?"

"Nothing happened to Cindy, Dave."

"I don't mean that," Dave said. "What if she died? You think I could forget that?"

Stanley's lips moved soundlessly. He could think of nothing to say.

"Sometimes I know that I go away, but when I come back I don't know where I went." Dave started to cry. He reached for a napkin and dabbed his eyes. "I'm scared that one day I'll go away and not come back."

"Dave . . ." Stanley began helplessly.

"Sometimes I know there's things I ought to know that I don't. And I don't know why. Like today. I don't know what day it is."

"It's Tuesday."

"But shouldn't I know that?"

Stanley shrugged. "I don't know. The days tend to blur for me, too."

"You know what happens sometimes, Stanley? I remember things from when I was younger and think they're what's going on now. That's funny, isn't it?" He pointed at Stanley's uneaten sandwich. "Getting cold."

"It's not meant to be hot." Stanley picked up the BLT with two hands and took a bite. His left hand began to shake. Stanley returned the sandwich to the plate and crossed his arms to ease the tremors.

"Sometimes it's as if I'm younger." Dave tapped at his head. "In here, I mean. You think that's what's happening? I'm getting younger?"

"Wouldn't that be something! But I know what you mean. There are days from my teens and twenties I remember like it was yesterday." He cleared his throat, not relishing what he was about to do. "Remember what you said this morning about Ronnie Dumat?"

"Who?" Dave had finished his cheeseburger and was working on the fries.

Stanley pulled the picture from his jacket pocket and passed it to Dave.

"Ronnie Dumat," Dave said.

"Remember what you told me?"

"What did I tell you?"

"Forget it." Stanley cleared his throat again. "Look at the picture. What do you remember about her?"

Dave looked carefully at the photograph. When he looked up at Stanley he was blushing. "I sure remember her tits," he said. "She had the greatest tits."

Stanley took back the photograph. The affirmation wasn't as painful as he had anticipated. "You know what, Dave? If I had to choose between remembering what day it is and what Ronnie Dumat's tits looked like, no contest."

As he tucked the photograph back in his jacket he heard "Jingle Bells" followed by a smirking voice booming, "Well, look who's here!" Stanley turned to see Birkholz walking toward the table, waving cheerfully, followed by Hustad. "Mind if we join you?" Birkholz asked, pulling out a chair without waiting for a reply.

Hustad walked around Dave and sat across from Birkholz. "Stopped by your office. Figured you might be here."

Stanley felt the blood drain from his face.

"Not going to say hello?" Birkholz asked. "You don't look all that happy to see us." He signaled Tracy and ordered two coffees.

"Say, as long as we're all together, why don't you tell them about Ed Lind?" Hustad said to Birkholz.

Birkholz lit a cigarette and waved his hand dismissively. "Oh, he probably knows." He squinted at Stanley. "Don't you?"

"Know what?" Stanley asked.

"That we tracked down Ed Lind."

After a moment's silence Stanley realized Birkholz was expecting him to say something. "How would I know that?"

"Maybe because he called you after we saw him?" Tracy placed cups before Birkholz and Hustad and filled them with regular. Birkholz tore open two plastic creamers and emptied them into the coffee, then two packages of sugar.

Stanley spread his hands. "I have no idea who this person is. And no, he didn't call me."

"Still sticking to the same old story, huh?"

"Honestly," Stanley said, "the name doesn't register at all."

"And that note we found? CALL ED LIND / JAMOS? You still say you have no idea what that's about?"

"I have no idea."

Birkholz hooked his thick finger in the coffee cup's ear, tilted his head back and drank half the cup. "Turns out Mr. Lind used to own an office supply company. Jefferson and Maxwell. That name ring a bell?"

"Jefferson and Maxwell?"

"That's what I said."

"Something about that seems familiar," Stanley said. "But I can't place it."

Birkholz blew a thick stream of smoke in Hustad's direction. "Ed Lind says he knows you real well. Says Jamos Company was his biggest customer. Says he was forced to shutter his company when yours went out of business." The gloating in Birkholz's voice was palpable. "Can you place that, maybe?" He downed the rest of his coffee and hoisted his cup in the air to signal Tracy for a refill.

"Look, detective, I don't care what this Ed Lind says. I don't know anybody by that name. And if he sold us office supplies, he would have been dealing with our office manager, not me. I had more important things to do than fill orders for paper clips."

"And maybe if you paid more attention to the paper clips you'd still be in business. But that's neither here nor there. Mr. Lind also turns out to be related to the vic. First cousins. Beginning to sound more familiar now?" Birkholz asked.

"Related to Vic? Who's Vic?"

"The victim. Mr. Tilden. And what he told us about doing business with you checked out. His company filed a claim in the Jamos Company bankruptcy. Big one, too." He sat back while Tracy refilled his cup. "You sure spent a lot of money on paper clips."

"*That* must be where I know Jefferson and Maxwell from," Stanley said. "The bankruptcy."

"Well, well. Progress. Here's another little tidbit for you. His company's claim is still unpaid."

Stanley shrugged. "So?"

Birkholz nodded to Hustad. "Read it to him."

Hustad held up his notebook. "My notes from Friday." He opened it to a tabbed page and started reading. " 'Q. What about the creditors? SJ.'—That's you, Mr. Jamos—'All paid except bank.' " He snapped the notebook shut.

"Seems you left out one unpaid creditor, Mr. Jamos," Birkholz said. "Which," he said, forming quotation marks with fingers, "coincidentally happens to be Jefferson and Maxwell Office Supplies, Incorporated."

Stanley experienced a wave of paranoia. *I'm a suspect,* he thought. He took a deep breath.

"Anything you want to tell us, Mr. Jamos?" Hustad prodded gently.

As firmly as he could, Stanley said, "Look, I never met this guy. And if his claim's still unpaid, it was an oversight. I thought we paid everyone except the bank."

"Well, here's what I'm thinking," Birkholz said cheerfully. "Mr. Lind asks his cousin—that would be Mr. Tilden—to help him out with the unpaid bill. Set up a meeting with you."

"He told you that?"

"The three of you get together," Birkholz continued, raising his voice to cut off Stanley. "Things get out of control. Someone pulls a gun. It goes off. Catches Mr. Tilden in the head." He paused, then continued, sounding conciliatory, almost apologetic. "Accidents do happen."

"If that's what it was," Hustad said, "I suggest you come clean with us sooner rather than later. We want to work with you. But our sympathy tends to dwindle the more time it takes us to make our case."

"Am I under arrest?" Stanley asked. The anxiety was triggering spasmodic twitching of his hand.

Birkholz dropped his cigarette butt in his coffee cup. "Let's just say I'm testing out theories here. I'm a theoretical thinker. You want another? You were observed having breakfast here yesterday with two men. And again today. Don't know who they are, but I got a feel for people. These two, they didn't strike me as, shall we say, in the office supply business. You want to tell us about them?"

"I'm under surveillance?"

Birkholz smirked. "This is a rough neighborhood, Mr. Jamos. We'd be derelict in our duty to the good citizens like you who work here if we didn't keep our eyes on it. So, you going to answer my question?"

"Their names are Doug and Tim," Stanley sighed. "I only met them yesterday. I don't even know their last names."

Doug and Tim, Hustad wrote. "Met them how?"

"They work around here. But their usual place for breakfast had a fire, so they ate here yesterday for the first time."

"And what? They just happened to strike up a conversation?"

"They wanted to know what was good. Nobody else in here to ask."

"That didn't strike you as odd? We find your partner's body on Friday? On Monday these two show up making"—Hustad cleared his throat—"culinary inquiries in . . . well, let's face it, calling this a greasy spoon would be an insult to greasy spoons."

Stanley shrugged. "I don't know. It never occurred to me. They didn't seem suspicious."

Hustad tossed his pen on the table, annoyed. "Oh, come on, Mr. Jamos. What kind of PI are you? Because all the PIs I know find everyone suspicious. Comes with the territory."

"One of them had a duffel bag yesterday," Birkholz said. "It sure looked a lot fuller when he carried it out than when he walked in. Like maybe it was filled with cash?"

"What are you suggesting?" Stanley asked.

"I'm suggesting some jobs, people don't take checks or credit cards. They want cash. Preferably small denominations."

"What? Are you saying I hired them to kill Pete?"

"You said it," Birkholz said. "I didn't."

"Or maybe they saw something you didn't want them talking about?" Hustad suggested.

Stanley started to rise. "That's it. Come on, Dave."

"Don't go far," Birkholz said. "In case we need to talk to you again. And you can be sure we'll be talking to Doug and Tim."

"You okay, Stanley?" Dave asked when they were back in the car. He pointed at Stanley's left hand. "Your hand's shaking."

Stanley drove back to the warehouse and spent the rest of the afternoon searching the desks and file cabinets and pawing through the rest of his company's debris. Just after four he called Ronnie at her hotel to report failure.

"Let's talk about it over dinner," she said. If she was disappointed by the news, her voice didn't convey it.

"There's not much to talk about, Ronnie."

"We have plenty to talk about." She named a recently opened Wicker Park restaurant. "I talked to some people who told me this is *the* place. Got them to pull some strings. Got a seven o'clock reservation."

Stanley knew Mary was at her afternoon book group. Based on experience they'd finish with an early dinner, which meant he could drop Dave off, go back to the apartment, shower and change and leave without risk of running into her. That was good. He felt awkward about her seeing him dressed up for another woman.

He called Cindy and told her he'd drive Dave home, then called Mary and got her answering machine.

"Hey Mary, it's Stanley," he began the message. "You won't believe this, but we just got hired to do an investigation. Anyway, I'm meeting the client for dinner, so I'll be back late." An image of Ronnie's breasts flashed through his mind. He thought, *Is this possible?* followed by, *Is this a stone I want turned over?*

He added, "Don't wait up. It might be real late."

CHAPTER 12

Stanley was on his third bourbon when Ronnie arrived at the restaurant. Shoulders hunched, glazed eyes staring listlessly at the swirls of wood in the bar, he didn't see her coming, and the music was so loud that he didn't hear her greeting. The tingle of her lips on his cheek caught him by surprise.

"Couldn't find anyplace noisier?" Ronnie asked. She waved at the bartender, ordered a dirty vodka martini, slipped off her fur and draped it over the back of the stool Stanley had saved for her. "Waiting long?"

"Ten, twenty minutes," Stanley said. Without turning to face her he slid an envelope her way. "I imagine you want this back."

"What's this?" With fingertips painted glossy pink—she'd had time for a manicure, Stanley observed—Ronnie opened the envelope and removed a five-thousand-dollar check to the order of R DUMAT drawn on the JAMOS & MOSIT, INC., PRIVATE INVESTIGATORS account. "What's the deal, Stanny?" she asked.

"I'm returning your money."

"Because?"

"I didn't earn it."

"Well, aren't you ethical?" Ronnie ripped the check into shreds and said, "I hate to break it to you, but your job is far from over."

"Ronnie, it wasn't there."

"Stanny." Her lips were taut and grim. "I have a huge com-

130

mission riding on this. I don't intend to lose it."

"But I looked . . ."

"Stanny," Ronnie interrupted. She stroked the back of Stanley's hand. "Come on. We have the whole night ahead of us. Let's take this in due time. Okay?"

Despite the casualness of the comment, *the whole night* tingled in Stanley's loins.

When the bartender brought Ronnie's drink he brought Stanley another bourbon, unsolicited. He also brought the tab, which he discretely placed equidistant between them. Ronnie intercepted it, glanced at the bill, tossed down three twenties and looked suspiciously at Stanley. "How many of those have you had?" she asked.

Stanley held up two fingers. "And a half," he said, holding up the glass he was drinking. "Not counting that," he added, nodding at the glass the bartender had just brought.

Ronnie shook her head. "That's too much. Certainly too much before dinner."

"Sometimes that's all I have for dinner," Stanley said. His words were drowned out by the music.

Ronnie hopped off the stool and picked up her glass. "This is too loud. You mind? I can hardly hear a word you're saying."

Stanley followed her to the fringe of the bar area where the music was less intrusive.

Ronnie nodded at the drink in Stanley's hand. "Should I be worried about you?"

"Should you be worried?" Stanley repeated reflectively, as if it were a deep philosophical inquiry. The honest answer was *Probably*, but that would invite a discussion Stanley didn't want. He was aware of his escalating dependency on alcohol and his periodic, ineffectual resolutions to stop or moderate. *None of your business* was heartfelt, but the belligerence risked jeopardizing the tantalizing possibilities lurking behind Ronnie's offhand *the whole night.* He could thwart further inquiry on the subject of alcohol with *I just found out you banged Dave in college,* but turning the rudder that hard was certain to take them into waters like those described on ancient maps by phrases like *There Be Monsters Here.* He could think of only one answer that was responsive yet, handled carefully, lead nowhere. It was neither the whole truth nor nothing but the truth, but it was the truth.

He extended his left hand and gave it an exaggerated shake. "Depression."

Ronnie watched the gesture solemnly. "That would depress anyone," she said.

"That's not what I mean. It's a biochemical side effect of the disease. The depression is caused by the loss of dopamine." He held his glass to the light. Speaking to the amber liquid, he said, "This is the most effective thing I've found for that. And for the tremors."

"Your doctor know how much you drink?"

Stanley nodded.

"Does he approve?" Ronnie asked skeptically.

"She calls alcohol a neurotoxin. Wants to put me on antidepressants. But with a disease like Parkinson's it's all guesswork."

"What's that supposed to mean, Stanny?"

"It means you go with what works. And this works for me."

Ronnie sighed. "I don't know, Stanny. I'm always suspicious of self-medication."

"Fair enough. I'm suspicious of doctors who prescribe mood-altering drugs." Stanley took one last swallow from glass number three and poured the remainder into number four. "Not to mention being lectured on drug use by a chain smoker."

"Touché," Ronnie said. "But it doesn't change the fact that I'm concerned."

The hostess approached, carrying two menus, and said, "Du-mat party? Please follow me."

Even without piped-in music the restaurant was louder than the bar. Tables were crammed into a chamber cleanly stripped of sound baffling. Noise ricocheted off the exposed brick, the carpetless hardwood floor, the barrel-sized metal ductwork suspended high overhead from broad wood beams. Diners conversed in shouts. Stanley began to ask Ronnie about her day as they were being seated, but a machine-gun burst of guffaws from the next table made Ronnie lean in and turn her head to position her ear to Stanley's mouth and ask, "What?"

"It wasn't important," Stanley said.

"It's worse here than in the bar," Ronnie complained.

"You want to leave? We can go somewhere else."

Ronnie gave the idea a passing thought, then shrugged. "It's only dinner. I guess we'll have to save the intimate conversation for after."

Intimate?

"Anyway, L.A.'s no better." She trickled olive oil onto her bread plate, sprinkled pepper over it, tore a piece of bread from the loaf, dipped it and placed it delicately on the tip of her tongue. "Though I'll tell you, I never got it. The attraction of places like this, where you can't even hear yourself think."

"If L.A.'s no better, what do you do?"

"I guess I'm a Santa Monica girl," Ronnie said. "You ever been there?"

"Just the beach," Stanley said. "Years ago."

She reached across the table and squeezed Stanley's hand. "You ought to go back there with me sometime. There's still cozy little places up and down Montana I can show you. A little on the precious side, I'll admit, doilies and lace curtains, but you can have a meal without overhearing everyone else." She looked to her left and to her right, frowning. "And them overhearing you."

"Never sell in Chicago," Stanley said. "We're built tough."

Ronnie leaned forward and asked, as quietly as she could and still be heard, "Doesn't anyone care about privacy?"

Before Stanley could respond the waitress appeared. Ronnie ordered an Oregon pinot noir and the waitress's three favorite appetizers. When she left, Stanley nodded over Ronnie's shoulder. "Turn around. Take a look at the guy a couple of tables behind. On your left."

Ronnie craned her neck.

"You see him? The one talking on the phone?" The man had a cell phone pressed to one ear, a finger stuffed into the other. His end of the conversation consisted largely of barking "What?" or "Can you hear me?" while his ignored dinner companion, a redhead several years his junior with large hoop earrings and tattoos circling her upper arms, studied the menu.

"What about him?" Ronnie asked as she turned back.

"When I was in the bathroom before you came he was in one of the stalls, talking on his cell phone. About the sex he had last night. And the quantity of coke they'd snorted."

"Stanny, you could have been a cop!"

"Or that girl's father. There wasn't a guy in there who couldn't hear every word."

Ronnie shrugged. "So he's a sociopath. What's your point?"

"My point, Ronnie, is that nobody cared. He's the normal one. Not you and me. People talking on cell phones will say anything at all in front of perfect strangers. As far as they're concerned, if you're not on the other end of their conversation, you can't hear what they're saying. And telephones, restaurants, it's all the same. If you're not at their table you don't exist."

The waitress brought the wine and stood by politely to confirm Ronnie's approval. Ronnie sniffed the cork, swirled the glass, inhaled, sipped, looked up at the waitress and nodded.

"You're making me feel old," Ronnie pouted. She picked up her glass, brought it to her lips and stared at Stanley over the rim. Her mascaraed lashes fluttered up and down with the sensuality of a butterfly slowly opening and closing its wings. Her blouse made no effort to conceal or every effort to reveal the tops of her breasts, a distinction that was becoming increasingly important to Stanley.

"You sure don't look old."

"You're sweet to say that."

The waitress returned with three plates, which she placed in the middle of the cramped table, describing each appetizer as she set it down.

"I still think of you as twenty," Ronnie said.

"You too, but at least you look the part."

"I look at you and I still see hair down to your shoulders."

"It's still there," Stanley said. "Except it's growing out of my ears."

Ronnie scooped half of the tuna tartare onto her bread plate. "Do you ever miss the sixties?"

Maybe he imagined it, but he heard in her question, *Do you ever miss me?* Stanley tried to spear an oyster, which was refusing to cooperate with the fork. "I miss how uncomplicated life was. Or seemed to be."

"Things definitely were more black and white," Ronnie agreed.

"I miss the fact that we were concerned about things like war and civil rights. I miss not being obsessed with bankruptcies and auctions."

"Amen to that. I hate the constant hustling."

"And I miss being able to eat with a fork," Stanley added.

"Well, that certainly puts it in perspective, doesn't it? Is it easier just to eat with your fingers? Go ahead. I won't mind."

"I'll manage," Stanley said, using a spoon to impale the oyster on the fork. "If you hate it so much, why not get out? It's none of my business, but don't you have enough money put away?"

Ronnie put her fork down. "I'll let you in on a secret, Stanny. I made up my mind. When this deal closes . . ."

"Homebase?"

Ronnie nodded. "I'm done."

"Wow," Stanley said. "I didn't realize you had that much riding on it."

"You can't imagine." For a moment Ronnie's gaze drifted off to the side, and went somewhere within. Then she smiled at Stanley. "It wasn't there?"

Stanley held up a thumb and forefinger, forming a zero. "Nothing."

"Where'd you look?"

"Everywhere." Ronnie sat silent and attentive as Stanley launched into an elaborate description of his search. He concluded, "I can't imagine an actual detective could have been more thorough."

Ronnie forked another oyster. "You wasted your time."

"What do you mean?"

"Why didn't you look in the files?"

"Ronnie," Stanley protested, "the warehouse is filled with files. Boxes and boxes of them. It would have been like looking for a needle . . ."

"The Homebase files," Ronnie interrupted.

"What?"

Ronnie set her fork on the plate, oyster still attached. "Stanny," she asked, exasperated, "what do you think Pete was doing there? Reviewing the Homebase files. Taking notes." She retrieved her fork and jammed the oyster in her mouth.

Stanley felt chastised. He could tell his cheeks were turning crimson. He stared uncertainly at the oyster he'd finally lured onto his fork. He shoved it in his mouth and began to chew. He swallowed, and felt himself begin to choke, his throat muscles spasming in confusion over whether to push the oyster down or send it back up, ending up alternating between both, swelling to a painful blockage in the process. Each time this happened, his immediate reaction was fear that he'd suffocate. Each time he had to test the apparatus, assure himself that his breathing was unimpaired, convince himself to remain calm until his muscles remembered how to relax and let the food pass. Before Ronnie could notice his discomfort the waitress appeared, asking, "Would you like to hear about tonight's specials?" By the time the presentation concluded the spasms had subsided enough to order.

"Well?" Ronnie asked when the waitress left with their orders.

"Well what?"

"The Homebase files are there. Aren't they?" She grabbed a knife and efficiently shepherded the last of her tuna tartare onto her fork.

"I assume so," Stanley said. "But why would he hide his notes there?"

Ronnie looked surprised by the question. "What makes you think he was hiding them? You really think he cared if anyone found them? What, and take them home for a little light reading before bed? Honestly, Stanny, you make it sound like Pete was engaged in some criminal activity. He was taking notes about a website he ran."

Stanley drummed his fingers on the tablecloth.

Ronnie set her knife and fork down and folded her hands. "You're still mad because he didn't tell you. Aren't you?"

"Damned right," Stanley snapped.

"Well, get over it," Ronnie said, returning to the oysters. "That's where you'll look tomorrow."

Stanley shook his head. "You should have come with. It would have saved us a lot of time."

Ronnie nodded. "You're probably right."

"So you'll come tomorrow?"

Ronnie reached across the table and patted Stanley's arm. "I wish I could. I am so snowed under."

"With other deals? I thought you said this one was going to be your last."

Ronnie refilled her glass. "My last new project. I still have others to close."

"What happens if I don't find the notes?"

Ronnie picked up her glass and shrugged.

"That kill the deal?"

Ronnie set her glass down and threw Stanley an admonishing look. "Are you serious?"

Stanley felt his face flush again, as if he'd been slapped.

"I'm surprised," Ronnie said. "I mean, you have more riding on this than I do. Why aren't you being more strategic?"

Stanley shook his head, dismayed. "What are you talking about?"

"All I get out of this is a commission. But every dollar Homebase brings in goes in your pocket. So why aren't you out there working to maximize the bid?"

"What am I supposed to do about it?"

Ronnie spread her hands, making no effort to hide her exasperation. "Be proactive. Make something happen. Look what Pete did. I mean, you're supposed to be the marketing guru, right? But it was Pete who was trying to jump-start the auction. And all you can think is, he was trying to screw you out of something. Tell me, Stanny. What do you think Homebase will go for?"

"Well, if it nets what we paid for it . . ."

Ronnie tossed her napkin on the table. "Get real, will you? This isn't a building. Or even a Picasso. It's a website. There's no market for it. Nobody's going to bid a penny."

Stanley felt the nausea build in his stomach. Her comment ripped the sheet off the simplistic illusion he'd built for himself that Homebase would sell for millions, fix everything, solve his financial problems.

"You've had nearly a year to create buzz for Homebase. I mean, was I wrong that that's what you used to do? Marketing?"

"I thought the auctioneer . . ."

"Forget the auctioneer, Stanny. Auctioneers don't generate interest. They don't do anything except take bids. Bang gavels. Talk fast."

"But the bid package . . ."

"You ever read one? Cookie-cutter crap. You know what they all say?"

Stanley stared at her blankly.

"Caveat emptor. That's what they say. You know how I spent my day?" Ronnie raised her glass and toasted Stanley. "I sold my boys on you running Homebase after they buy it."

"Ronnie, what are you talking about?"

"What do you think I'm talking about? Half of them were ready to walk after Pete's murder. They bargained for him to run it, and when they heard . . ."

"I thought this whole issue was Pete's notes."

Ronnie sighed, frustrated. "The issue, Stanny, is sales. My God, if anyone should understand that, you should. They wanted Pete because I sold him to them. His presentation was the icing on the cake, but they were already hooked. And today I turned it around. Now I've got them all psyched up on the idea of you running it."

"Ronnie," Stanley said, "that makes no sense. Any headhunter can get them a hundred people more qualified."

Ronnie rested her right elbow on the table, cupped her cheek in the palm of her hand and looked at Stanley. The gesture sang

to him from forty years away. It took a moment to place. Then
he remembered. He'd catch her looking at him that way when
he was doing homework. It was one of her many signals that
she wanted to be taken to bed. "You really don't get it, do you?
What I do for a living?"

"You told me. You're a broker. You introduce people with
money to people with projects."

"You make it sound like I run a dating service. You think
that's all I do? Make the introduction, send them off to a movie
and call the next morning to see how it went? I'm in sales,
Stanny. I make the investors drool for the project. That's how I
earn my commission. You get it? Sure, they can call a headhunter
and get a CEO. But only I can sell them you. Because that's
what I do, Stanny. I create demand."

Stanley reached for his wine glass and turned it slowly on the
tablecloth. "So you told them about me?"

"Damned straight."

He tapped his fingers against the glass. "Should I ask what
you said?"

"Nothing that wasn't the truth."

"And they want me?"

"They're desperate to get you."

"Is there an offer?"

"Same as Pete. Equity, salary, perks."

"So the only thing left," Stanley said coyly, "is selling me on
taking the job."

Ronnie grinned. "That's the beauty of it, Stanny. You'll sell
yourself." She reached across the table and squeezed Stanley's
hand. "There's no buzz out there for Homebase, Stanny. Trust
me. I've made inquiries. You blow them off, they don't bid. And
if they don't bid, the only people who'll show up at the auction
will be the bottom feeders. You got no choice here, Stanny. It's
heads you win, tails you lose. There's no in between."

Stanley took a drink of water. The Parkinson's had a tendency to make him drool, while the medication made his mouth dehydrated. In a just world the two would neutralize, but instead he alternated from one to the other. "I have no operational experience with Homebase. I've never negotiated a website licensing or advertising deal. I'd have no idea what to do."

Ronnie shrugged. "So hire yourself someone who does. Learn on the job."

Stanley thought about the salary. He thought about the benefits. He thought about how he'd endured the past two years without them. "So none of this had anything to do with finding Pete's notes, did it? This was just to see if I was a plausible substitute for Pete?"

"Not at all. I came here to find Pete's notes. My boys were really desperate to see them. Selling them on you was a backup."

"They still want to see Pete's notes?"

"You bet."

"And if I don't find them, you'll sell them on something else?"

Ronnie grinned. "You're finally catching on."

"What?"

"How many steps ahead would you like to know?" She batted her eyelashes. "Here's the first. We sit them down with the people who sold Homebase to you."

"You don't need me for that . . ." Stanley began. Then he understood. "No. You do. Because the sellers signed a confidentiality agreement."

Ronnie winked.

Stanley's eyes narrowed. "Is that the real reason you sold your investors on me? Because God forbid Pete's notes don't show up, I'm the only person who can get our sellers to talk to them?"

"Stanny, why are you so cynical?" Ronnie squeezed his hand

again. "Don't you get it? This is a win-win. Lemons into lemonade."

"Be straight with me, Ronnie. Would you have pushed me if it weren't for the confidentiality agreement?"

"You want a straight answer?"

Stanley nodded.

"Okay. The fact that I can't get your sellers to do a dog and pony without you is a deal point, no question about it. The rest of you is pluses and minuses."

"The fact that I have Parkinson's?"

Ronnie waved away the concern. "The crowd I run in? Not even a factor. Maybe even a plus. One of my biggest investors has it, too. He raises a ton of money for research. He's working with the Michael J. Fox Foundation to take it out of the closet. Make it an 'in' disease. The next AIDS. Or breast cancer."

"What, then?"

"Your biggest plus is the fact that you own Homebase. Your biggest minus is that you didn't run it."

"Hardly sounds like much of a compelling case for me," Stanley said.

"Don't get so hung up on the details," Ronnie said. "They don't matter. It's like I told you last night. You're the only person for the job."

"You just didn't tell me what the job was."

"Sometimes," Ronnie said, "you have to let the story unfold to make the sale. Hell, Stanny, you of all people ought to know that." She gave Stanley's hand another squeeze.

Stanley studied her hand, resting so lightly on his. "I haven't said yes."

"But you will." Ronnie said. "You know it, and I know it."

A busboy cleared away the appetizer plates. The waitress appeared followed by a server carrying a tray with the entrees. Ronnie ordered another bottle of pinot noir and sampled her salmon. "Nice," she declared. "Not Napa, but nice."

"Is Napa Valley the home of the food god or something?" Stanley asked, annoyed.

"No, Stanny, Napa Valley is not the home of the food god," Ronnie replied, spitting his words back at him. "It's just one standard to measure good living. And that's what I'm trying to offer you. I'm not saying after what you've been through you should be grateful, but . . ." She shook her head. "I give up."

Stanley slowly rotated his wine glass while Ronnie was speaking. A burst of laughter came from behind her after she finished, but he heard it as if from a great distance. He stared at his half-eaten entree and pushed it aside. He raised his glass and took a sip. He looked at Ronnie and said, "When I said I haven't said yes, I meant it."

Ronnie placed her fork delicately on her plate and folded her hands. "Nobody's forcing you, Stanny," she said. Her eyes boring into his undermined the casualness with which she added, "It's only money."

"I know," Stanley said. "Isn't that the bitch."

The waitress brought and uncorked the new bottle and refilled their glasses. "What's on your mind?" Ronnie asked, ignoring the waitress's question about the quality of their entrees.

"The thought of getting back into the rat race."

"Look, you know I have a personal interest in this, so I won't pretend to be objective," Ronnie said. "Even so, it seems so obvious to me. I mean, what choice do you have?"

Stanley tapped his fingers on the table. He took another sip of wine. He tapped his fingers some more. He looked at Ronnie. "Would there be a place for Dave?"

"You're a good person, Stanny," Ronnie said. "You're the CEO. You can hire anyone you want."

"As long as we're making lemonade, might as well make a lot," Stanley said.

CHAPTER 13

After dinner they strolled along Milwaukee Avenue, bundled up against the March night, pausing to look in the windows of the boutiques and art galleries. Ronnie suggested the walk, then apologized, asking if she was being insensitive to what she called his condition.

"I just move slowly," Stanley said brusquely. "I don't have a broken leg."

Half a block down Ronnie turned into a gallery exhibiting Haitian art. Pedestals displayed small toy buses and cars and airplanes and larger free-form designs crafted from aluminum cans, brightly painted and then adorned with glued-on trinkets and glitter. The walls were hung with tapestries made of threaded sequins and paintings of tropical jungles with tigers and parrots and women carrying baskets on their heads. They were alone save for a clerk, an early-twenties female with spiked purple and green hair and a ring through her nose and another through her lower lip, neither of which was any match for the artillery sprouting from her ears and a tattoo of a sunburst above her left breast. She was reading a paperback, showed no interest in them when they entered and did not show any as they walked from item to item.

"Do you like these?" Ronnie asked.

Stanley nodded. "Yeah, I do. Though I don't pretend to know much about art, unless you count graphic design."

"That you do pretend to know about?" Ronnie asked, punching Stanley playfully in the arm. She abruptly walked away and picked up a brochure about the exhibition.

"You can keep it," the clerk said disinterestedly, snapping her gum.

"Thanks," Ronnie said. She folded the brochure and stuffed it in her purse and started walking toward the clerk, pointing at a toy airplane and asking, "Can you tell me how much . . ." when a cell phone chirped. The clerk flipped it open, held it to her ear and answered with a shout loud enough to be heard on the street, "Hey, babe!"

Stanley looked at Ronnie. She looked at him. They eye-signaled the door. As they exited, Ronnie pulled the folded brochure from her purse and tossed it into the garbage can.

They continued west, Ronnie's pace slowing as she checked window displays. She stopped again at a clothing boutique catering to teenage girls. The dummies loitered insouciantly in clothes displaying bare plastic midriffs and tops of breasts.

"You wear these?" Stanley asked skeptically.

"My niece does," Ronnie said. "My sister calls the style, 'Hi, I'm Susie and these are my boobs.' "

"Might work as a slogan. It certainly nails down the concept."

Ronnie walked in and fingered a blouse. "Forty years later and I can still fit into these," she said. "The problem is, who'd want to?"

"Your niece, for one."

"Not at her weight." She rotated the rack.

Stanley put a hand tenderly on Ronnie's forearm. "You sorry you never had children?"

"I don't think I would have made a good mother," she said without making eye contact. "And in answer to your next question, no."

"No what?"

"I don't think I would have made a good wife, either."

"Why not?"

"Some things weren't meant to be."

They left the store. Ronnie resumed walking at the same snail's pace. Outside a coffee shop, Stanley said, more curtly than he'd intended, "You want to know something? A man with Parkinson's walks faster than a woman who's window shopping."

"Very funny," Ronnie deadpanned. She jerked her purse open and pulled out a pack of cigarettes. "Would you mind getting me a green tea and honey?" she asked as she lit up.

A moment later Stanley came out with two cups. He handed one to Ronnie, took a deep breath and without looking at her asked, "Why did we break up?"

Ronnie showed no outward sign of discomfort at the question. Gingerly testing the tea she said, "I wonder about that myself every now and then." She put a hand on his coat sleeve. Surely it was imagined, but he felt warmth on the spot she so lightly touched. "I thought we were lovers. And then one day you broke up with me. At least that's how I remember it."

Stanley shut his eyes. *One day.*

The day he ended it.

He remembered it vividly. He had relived it many times, and had tried not to think about it many more times.

He went to her apartment to give her a note. It wasn't long. It ended, *I don't want to see you again.* She opened the door. He said nothing, just handed the note to her. He stood in her doorway as she removed it from the envelope and began to read. Then he turned and walked away. He didn't look back, afraid to see the expression on her face. He would have been relieved to see surprise, shock, confusion, even anger. But he would have been devastated to see what his intuition told him he'd see: a cold, mocking sneer.

He wanted her to call his name and plead with him to come

back. He wanted to turn and tell her he didn't mean it and apologize. Neither happened.

After graduating he returned home to Chicago to enter his father's business, Dave and Pete in tow. He assumed she left Madison for Hollywood, to fulfill her dream of becoming an actress. He didn't see or hear from her again, not until her out-of-the-blue call the day before.

"Ronnie," he said, "I couldn't take the rejection."

She turned away. He saw no tears in her eyes, but she looked on the verge of crying. Or perhaps, he speculated, he wanted to see tears. Perhaps to justify to himself that his disease was the appropriate punishment for how he'd mistreated her.

"Stanny," she said. "You rejected me."

"Because you stopped having sex with me. Don't you remember that?"

"It was a long time ago, Stanny."

"Not to me. One day you just stopped having sex with me. You wouldn't tell me if it was anything I said or did. You just wouldn't let me touch you. I was going out of my mind. Finally, I realized there was only one thing left for me to do with dignity. And that was it."

"Why didn't you say something? Ask?"

"I was afraid of what you might have said. Afraid I wouldn't be able to handle it."

She put her hand on his sleeve. "That was how I felt."

Stanley felt adrift. He felt his arm begin to shake. He pitched his nearly full decaf into a garbage can and said, "I think I need a real drink."

Ronnie dropped her tea in the garbage as well. "I think I do too."

Stanley pointed to a bar across the street. "Okay?"

"It does have the advantage of proximity."

They crossed the street. Inside Stanley helped Ronnie with

her fur. He ordered a bourbon for himself, a dirty vodka martini for her. They sat in a booth. After an awkward silence Stanley asked, "Where did we go wrong?"

Ronnie toyed with her martini glass. "Maybe things turned out the way they were supposed to."

"You really believe that?"

"I don't know what to think," Ronnie said. She sipped at her drink, pushed it away and covered a yawn with the back of her hand.

"You ready to call it a night?" Stanley asked.

Ronnie reached into her purse, pulled out a lipstick and dabbed color on her lips. "You mind driving back to the hotel with me?"

And then . . . ? Stanley thought. He said, "Not at all."

They caught a taxi back to the Loop. When they got in, Ronnie squeezed Stanley's thigh and said, "I am so ready for bed." With that, she rested her head on his shoulder and shut her eyes.

They rode in silence.

By the time the taxi pulled up, Stanley had explored so many permutations of what could happen that he could think of nothing to say.

Ronnie pre-empted his quandary. She kissed him lightly on the mouth and said, "You want to come up?"

Ronnie pushed ahead of Stanley when the elevator let them out on her floor. She opened the door to her room and stopped to let Stanley in first. In the periphery of his vision he saw her put the DO NOT DISTURB card on the doorknob as she closed it.

The drapes were open. Ronnie's room faced east and north. Stanley walked to the window and looked down at State Street and the taillights of cars heading toward River North.

"Can I get you anything?" Ronnie opened the mini-bar and

looked inquisitively at Stanley. "Bourbon? Or a really nice Sirah I brought from home?"

"Wine sounds great."

"It's on the nightstand. Pour one for me, too. Excuse me for a moment." She disappeared into the bathroom.

An uncorked, nearly full bottle and two wine glasses were on the stand by the king-sized bed. Stanley filled them. He picked up one, brought it to his lips and turned.

The bathroom door was partially open. Ronnie's back was reflected in the mirror on the door. She was leaning over the sink, applying lipstick. She'd taken off her skirt and blouse and was wearing only stockings, panties, and a brassiere. As Stanley watched she reached her left hand behind her back, unclipped her brassiere and slipped it off her left shoulder. Propriety told him to turn away, but lust prevailed.

Ronnie caught sight of Stanley watching her. The hand holding the lipstick stopped moving. She set the tube on the sink. Her back still to Stanley but her eyes staring at his reflection in the mirror, she slipped the brassiere off the right shoulder. It dropped to the floor.

She turned.

Her breasts were uplifted, larger than he remembered. Firm. Hoops dangled from pierced nipples. Her tummy was flat, tight, without stretch marks.

She stepped through the bathroom door and paused. "Can I have my wine now, please?" she asked, no hint of emotion or arousal in her voice.

Stanley turned, stooped, picked up her wine glass and turned back.

Ronnie had advanced into the room. Metal handcuffs dangled from her right hand. "Bring it to me," she said.

Stanley's left hand began to quiver. Wine sloshed out of the glass. He took a hesitant step toward her.

Ronnie looked at the red stain on the carpet, shook her head disapprovingly and with two firm strides closed the gap between them. "Hold these," she said, arching her breasts up as she held out the handcuffs and took her glass, her expression coyly refusing to resolve the ambiguity of what, precisely, he was being asked to hold.

Stanley's hand moved tentatively toward her breasts, then descended abruptly and seized the handcuffs.

"Don't you like my nipple rings?" Ronnie asked.

Stanley's hand jerked, the handcuffs snapping with the motion.

"Go on," Ronnie urged.

Stanley hesitantly raised his hand until his fingers hovered at the ring piercing her left nipple.

"Touch it," Ronnie said.

Stanley crooked his forefinger into the ring. He pulled at it tentatively. The nipple resisted.

"Harder," Ronnie pleaded.

Stanley tugged. The nipple stretched forward, resistant but yielding. He knew she was feeling pain. He knew she liked it.

"Pinch it," Ronnie said.

Stanley released the ring, grabbed the nipple, and squeezed.

Ronnie shut her eyes. "Hurt me," she said.

Stanley squeezed harder. A lopsided smile grew on Ronnie's face. She began to hum softly. "Good," she said. She held up her wrists in submission. "Let's play a game. Cuff me to the bed."

What's happening? Stanley thought, followed, with a sobering jolt, by *Mary!*

He released her nipple.

"I can't," Stanley said. "Please forgive me. I can't." He set the wine glass on the dresser, opened the door and left, dread-ing what would happen if Ronnie followed and begged him to come back.

When the elevator door chimed and opened, he practically fell in. The ground floor button was already lit but he jabbed at it several times anyway, then sagged against the rear wall of the cage, feeling wholly depleted. The two passengers gave him a strange look and edged away. He assumed it was because his arm was shaking.

He didn't realize until he was outside the hotel and flagging down a cab that he was still holding the handcuffs.

CHAPTER 14

Stanley rapped lightly on Mary's door. No response. He glanced at his watch. Eleven-thirty. He started to knock again but froze before his fist hit the door, his desperate need for release momentarily winning the tug of war with the downright un-gentlemanliness of using Mary to quench his lust for Ronnie. Propriety seized control. He dropped his hand and walked away.

Halfway to the elevator he heard behind him the sound of a door opening.

"I thought that was you," Mary said groggily. "Why are you leaving?"

"It didn't seem fair."

"Fair?" Mary asked, perplexed.

Because I was unfaithful to you, he thought, *even if only in my mind.* "I mean polite. To wake you," he said as he turned and walked back to her apartment.

"I would have been delighted to be awakened," she said. "Besides, I finished it. Come see." She crooked her arm around his. "On the table."

He'd watched Mary toil at it for weeks. Buckingham Fountain, the colossal water fountain in the center of Grant Park on Lake Shore Drive. On summer nights it became a colored light show, a concrete-and-water replication of a mescaline-induced hallucination.

Her needlepoint was crude. The fountain lacked depth. The colors were flat.

Stanley said, "It's really nice."

Mary laughed. "No it's not. But it's yours."

"Mine? Why?"

"For your office. To celebrate your first case." She flopped onto the couch and patted an invitation on the cushion for him to sit next to her. "Come and tell me all about it."

"Well," he began, and decided, *I might as well come out with it.* "For starters, the client is my old college girlfriend. I haven't seen or talked to her in forty years. Showed up out of the blue." He tossed his overcoat on the back of a chair and sat next to her.

"Ooh!" Mary said, her mouth a circle of concern. "Old girlfriends can be dangerous!"

"Seems Pete . . ."

"The Pete who was murdered?"

". . . was working with her to buy a website Jamos Company owns," Stanley continued. "She's a broker. Pete told her she should put a group together to buy it."

"Hmm," Mary said. "And what was Pete going to get out of it?"

"You picked up on that quickly," Stanley said, impressed.

Mary shrugged. "It didn't sound like a charitable endeavor."

"Some ownership of the website. And they'd hire him to run it."

"Hmm." She looked closely at Stanley. "Let me guess. This came as news to you?"

Stanley nodded. "You picked up on that one, too."

"Old girlfriends don't show up out of the blue, as you put it, to tell you something you already know."

"Pete was preparing a presentation for her investors. He was murdered before he delivered it. Ronnie hired me to help her find it."

"That's her name? Ronnie?"

Stanley nodded.

"Who were her parents? The Ronettes?"

"Very funny."

Mary casually rested her hand on Stanley's thigh. "Don't take this personally, Stanley, but why not a real detective?"

"I had the same question. But she didn't really need a detective as much as access to our Bensenville building where Pete was working on it."

"And did you find it?"

Stanley shook his head. "Not yet. I'll go back tomorrow and keep looking."

"So you really *are* being a detective?"

"I guess you could say that."

Mary squeezed Stanley's knee and rose. "And your very first case is a murder mystery, too. You sure you know what you're getting yourself into?"

"Isn't that a little melodramatic?" Stanley asked Mary's back as she bounced into the kitchen.

Mary emerged carrying a bottle of bourbon and two small glasses and dropped back on the couch. "Guess it depends on whether there's any connection between the murder and what Pete was working on."

"He was murdered by robbers."

"Well, I certainly make it sound more interesting. Or is that speaking ill of the dead?" She filled two glasses and handed one to Stanley.

"I've had so much to drink tonight I feel my blood's been replaced by alcohol," Stanley said. He took a small sip and felt the fiery liquid attack the back of his throat. It made no dent in his unyielding sobriety.

Mary set the bottle on the floor. "So you went to dinner with your old girlfriend?"

Stanley nodded. "And last night, too. That was when she hired me."

"The plot thickens." Mary frowned. "I wondered what happened to you. Is she pretty?"

"Looks the same as she did in college," Stanley said.

At this, Mary took a big drink of bourbon. "You couldn't lie and tell me she's all wrinkled and gray?" She pouted, wiping her lips with the back of her hand.

"I could have," Stanley said. "Except you'll see her at Pete's funeral, and then you'd really accuse me of lying."

"Would have bought you a couple more days of domestic tranquility," Mary said with a wink. "You think they were romantically involved? Ronnie and Pete?"

A wave of nausea overcame Stanley. He began to cough.

"I'll take that as a yes." Mary moved a cushion to the arm of the couch and repositioned herself so that her feet, covered in furry slippers in the shape of bunnies, rested on Stanley's lap. "So where'd you go for dinner?"

Stanley named both restaurants.

"I've heard of them," Mary said. She crossed her arms. "Do I have to hire you to get you to take me there? Because if so, I could use your help. My boyfriend went missing."

"Come on, Mary, she took me. Expense account." He pulled off Mary's slippers and began massaging her feet.

"Pretty and rich, too. Guess I know where I stand." She watched with amusement as Stanley began to flounder for an explanation and cut him off with a quick kiss on the lips. "I'm just teasing you, Stanley. Don't be so serious."

Stanley's fingers moved up to Mary's ankles. "I am serious."

"Hey! Don't stop with the feet." When Stanley resumed massaging her arches Mary sighed contentedly. "You ought to get someone to give you a massage. Help you lighten up."

"I can't help it, Mary. I had an epiphany tonight."

Mary batted her eyelashes. "So she's pretty and rich and gives good epiphany?"

"Look," Stanley snapped, "just because you've never lost everything . . ." The words came out of their own volition. He was startled and appalled to hear them, as if they were the words of an offending stranger. Reflexively he clamped his hands over his mouth. "My God, Mary, I didn't mean that the way it sounded."

But Mary didn't seem put off. She reached for his hands and sternly placed them back on her feet. "I understand what you mean, Stanley. You mean I never suffered the kind of financial reversal you had. More to the point, you mean my sense of self-worth isn't so tied up in how much money I have that if I did lose it . . . Here." Mary reached down for the bottle and refilled his glass. "Try to relax."

I could love this woman, Stanley thought. He took another sip. "You know, when Dave and I got sick, Pete and Dave and I agreed we'd sell the company. We spent our lives building it up and thought of it as our retirement plan. We never actually had it valued. We just assumed it would be worth a fortune. So we hired a consulting firm to tell us what we could get. Do the marketing. Find us a buyer. But when they looked at our books, they said our finances were too unorthodox. Our clients were such big businesses that they played by their own rules. It was typical for our invoices to be outstanding for half a year or longer. Since we always got paid, we never considered it a problem. But we weren't thinking in terms of how it would look to a buyer."

"Must have been a rude awakening." Mary wiggled her toes.

"To say the least," Stanley agreed, switching from her arches to her toes. "They said based strictly on the books, with our stale receivables, we'd be lucky if we got three million." He cleared his throat. "They also said, as diplomatically as they could, that some of the prospective buyers would lowball because of my illness. Claim it devalued the post-closing consultation agreement, since they didn't know if I'd be functional enough to transition my knowledge of the business."

Mary scowled. "If it were me and a buyer insulted me that way, I'd tell them to look somewhere else. Anyway, three million? Sounds like a lot to me."

"Not when we'd been counting on getting ten times that. So we dumped the consultant and came up with our own strategies to position the company for sale. As luck would have it, the website I was mentioning came on the market just after we got the consultant's report. Seemed like a brilliant strategic move, and it was only ten million . . ."

"Dollars?" Mary asked, shocked.

"In the world of e-commerce, that's nothing."

"To you, maybe. But I don't understand. How could they say you were worth only three million dollars if you had ten million lying around?"

"We didn't. We had to borrow it."

"Oh." Mary took another sip. "I don't pretend to know much about selling a business, but if I was doing it, I don't think I'd consider spending that much money prudent."

"Well, in hindsight you're right. The loan was what ultimately buried us. What can I say? We got greedy."

"That was your epiphany?" Mary asked.

Stanley took another swallow. "No," he said, starting to feel woozy. "Tonight we were in this restaurant. The newest place to see and be seen. I was looking at everyone and they all had the same expression. Radiant smile and vacant eyes. The blissed-out look you only get if you don't have a financial care in the world, if you never worry where your next dollar is coming from. That or you're in some transcendent Zen state. You know what I mean, Mary?"

Mary prodded Stanley's hands with her big toe. "Only when you're giving me a massage."

"You don't get that way because you can buy anything you want. You only get that way when you feel you're entitled to it. I looked at them and realized, they all think they deserve the money they have. If not because they're better than everyone else—which is probably how they all feel, anyway—then because they're better at making money than everyone else. Which is exactly the way I used to feel before I fell flat on my ass. But you see? That's just an illusion. The reality is that the people who have money have it because they're just lucky. Because things worked out for them. Because money doesn't care who owns it. And they'll never understand that until they get kicked flat on their ass and end up asking, where the hell did that come from?"

"So that was your epiphany," Mary said.

"No." Stanley was beginning to slur his words and his eyelids were sagging, the sobriety finally dissipating. "I realized I never want to be like them. Never again."

"Oh," Mary said. "So *that* was the epiphany."

"And then Ronnie offered me a job. Her investors want to hire me to run the website if they buy it. More or less the same deal they were willing to make with Pete. Even give Dave a job."

"Dave?" Mary said skeptically. "Sounds too good to be true."

"And I realized that if I could get back my old lifestyle . . ."

"If you could become just like the very people you'd sworn only seconds ago . . ."

"You got it," Stanley said. "I realized that whatever deal I'd have to make with the devil to get there—"

"You'd make in a heartbeat."

Stanley raised his glass in a mock toast. "And *that* was my epiphany. My God, Mary. Have I always been this shallow?"

"Not since I've known you," Mary said. "But have no fear.

Shallowness never forgets. It's like riding a bike." She swung her feet off Stanley's lap. "You know what your problem is? You've been corrupted by money. From what I understand, that's a road that once taken, it's not so easy to get off. Now, me, I've never had the opportunity to be corrupted. But I'm willing to learn. So my recommendation is, take the job, make millions, and get us both out of here." She hoisted her glass. "I'll drink to *that.*" She downed the bourbon, stared at the empty glass and said, "Look what you've done, Stanley. You turned me into an alky."

"Mary . . . ?"

Mary put her fingertip on Stanley's lips and said, "I know. You want to get laid."

"Desperately," Stanley admitted.

Mary took Stanley's hand and started to stand. "Next time you see this Ronnie, you be sure to thank her for me for getting you so horny. That's one thing old girlfriends are always good for. But I warn you, Stanley. You call out her name, you better be doing a Ronettes karaoke."

"Promise," Stanley said.

"And what I said about old girlfriends being dangerous? I meant it."

"I'll keep it in mind," Stanley said.

"No you won't. And the rest of it? The job and all? Try not to dwell on it."

"Why's that, Mary?" Stanley asked as he moved toward the bedroom.

"Because when things seem too good to be true, it's usually because they are. Trust me on that one."

Stanley gave Mary a salute.

"Meet you in bed," Mary said. "I'm going to straighten up." She picked up Stanley's overcoat and the bottle and glasses.

Stanley went into the bedroom, undressed and flopped on

the bed, naked. A moment later Mary appeared in the door, a bemused smile on her face.

"What's so funny?" Stanley asked.

Eyes twinkling, Mary held up the handcuffs and said, "Really. You shouldn't have."

★ ★ ★ ★ ★

WEDNESDAY

★ ★ ★ ★

CHAPTER 15

Morning arrived in Bensenville with blue sky and a blazing sun in combat with the frigid air.

When Stanley began searching the files, time seemed frozen. Nothing moved except the dust motes floating languidly in the shafts of sunlight streaming in through the warehouse windows. Dave, sitting nearby, was so motionless that he could have been a statue. In the unearthly quiet Stanley could scarcely hear his own breathing. He felt a chill run down his spine and thought, *Pete's ghost is haunting me.*

In less than ninety minutes Stanley was through.

He began by identifying which of the cardboard boxes stacked head-high and running the length of a wall to open. Armed with a pad of neon green stickers, he worked his way from left to right, reading the contents descriptions and tagging any box with HOMEBASE written on it. When he was done, he had stickered precisely one box. According to the notation it contained files on both HOMEBASE PURCHASE and RE-PAIRS / MAINTENANCE.

He carried the box to a desk, wheeled a chair over, sat and removed the lid.

About a third of the box was folders containing the minutiae of property ownership. Insurance binders. HVAC maintenance agreements. Contracts for scavenger and snow-plowing services. Bids for a roof replacement. The rest was taken up by the three bound closing books from the Homebase acquisition, leaving room for two slim manila folders, one labeled HOMEBASE ACQUISITION—CORRESPONDENCE and a second labeled HOMEBASE ACQUISITION—DRAFTS.

No yellow legal pads.

Stanley removed the closing books and the folders and placed them on the desk.

He looked through the closing books first, skimming the acquisition, consultation and non-competition agreements, looking for the sellers' contact information, tabbing relevant pages with stickers. Next he opened the CORRESPONDENCE and DRAFTS folders and read every entry. When he finished, he sat back and propped his feet up on the desk and rested his eyes.

When he opened his eyes a few minutes later and looked outside the windows, the sky was cloudy. Stanley pulled out his cell phone, called information and asked for Ronnie's hotel. Connected, he asked to be put through to a guest, Ronnie Dumat.

A moment later he heard Ronnie ask, "Hi, Stanny. Where are you?" Her voice was so cheerful, Stanley wondered for an instant if the previous night had been a dream.

"At the warehouse."

After giving him a moment to speak she cued, "Well?"

"There's nothing here."

"What do you mean, nothing?"

"Closing books. Some letters. That's about it."

"No yellow legal pads?"

"Not a one."

After a pause, Ronnie said, "I guess Pete must have been working out of his house."

"That's the way it looks," Stanley agreed.

"Damn! I sure got that wrong." Another pause. "Looks like we may have to kiss his analysis goodbye." Her sigh was audible over the telephone. "You ready to call the sellers?"

Stanley cleared his throat to ease the hoarseness. "I hate to say it, Ronnie, but there's a problem there, too. I looked through everything for their telephone number. I didn't even find a street address. Just a post office box in the Bahamas."

"What about email?"

"Nothing. Just the PO box."

"Then we'll contact their attorney."

"Yeah, I thought about that. Except I didn't find anything with the attorney's name or address or telephone number either."

"Not even correspondence?"

"Zip," Stanley said.

"Can't say as I'm all that impressed with your record keeping," Ronnie said. "Okay. Your attorney probably has the sellers' phone numbers. Call him . . ."

"Her," Stanley corrected.

"Call her and find out. No, wait. Those numbers could be old. Better get the name and number of the sellers' attorney, too. And also their accountant. Oh, yeah, and their banker. Attorneys and accountants come and go, but banks are forever. We'll work from there. Get back to me?"

After hanging up with Ronnie, Stanley scrolled down to Anna Nelson's number. She answered on the second ring.

"Hi, Anna. It's Stanley Jamos."

"Mr. Jamos," Anna boomed. "How are you doing?" Her regular speaking voice was decibels above normal. On speakerphone, she was deafening. Stanley held his cell phone a few inches from his ear.

"Ups and downs, Anna. Ups and downs. How about you?"

"The usual. Trying to keep my clients out of trouble. I'm glad you called. You were on my list."

"What about?"

"Homebase. There's some details to take care of since Mr.

Tilden . . ." She left the sentence unfinished.

"That's exactly what I was calling about," Stanley said. "Homebase. I was hoping you could give me some names and telephone numbers. The sellers. Their attorney. Their accountant. And their banker."

"Sure. Hold on a second." Stanley heard the click of a temporary disconnection. Then Anna came back. "I just told my secretary to bring me the files. I'll pull what's there. And if you don't mind, could you stop by here this afternoon? So we can discuss a few things?"

"Not a problem," Stanley said.

"How's three o'clock?"

"Three works."

After disconnecting he swung his legs off the desk and announced, "Let's get some lunch." Dave stood immediately, as if he'd been expecting just such an invitation.

Stanley closed and locked the building. The temperature had dropped at least fifteen degrees since they arrived. They drove to a nearby restaurant and ate in silence.

CHAPTER 16

Stanley and Dave were ushered into a fifteen-by-fifteen conference room furnished with a table, four chairs and a telephone. The thirty-second floor window faced west, presenting a dizzying panorama of Chicago. The Sears Tower dominated the view on the left. To the far northwest, circling jets marked the location of O'Hare Airport. Stanley figured he could see the Bensenville warehouse if he knew where to look.

An assistant brought regular coffee for Dave and decaf for Stanley. She reached for Dave's hat, offering to put it in the reception area closet with his overcoat. Dave defiantly clamped his hands on the brim. The assistant shrugged and left. From outside the room Stanley heard her mutter, "Asshole."

Anna entered a moment later, carrying a thin file, a legal pad and a glass of ice water. She dropped the file on the table and extended her hand to shake Stanley's. "Sorry I'm late," she apologized as she sat. "Couldn't get off the phone. Nice to see you, Mr. Jamos. You too, Mr. Mosit. I still can't get over what happened to Mr. Tilden."

"None of us can," Stanley said.

"So tragic." She shook her head. "Such a nice man. Walked in on a robbery, from what I hear."

"That's what the police seem to think," Stanley said.

Dave reached for his coffee and asked Anna, "Pete was robbed?"

"And murdered," Stanley said.

Dave set the cup down on the lip of the saucer. Anna reached over and centered the cup before any coffee could spill out. "He didn't have insurance?"

"Why do you keep asking about his insurance?" Stanley asked. But by the time he'd craned his neck around to look at Dave, Dave's eyes were shut.

Anna looked at Stanley, flickered her eyes to Dave and back, and arched her eyebrows, communicating *How's he doing?*

Stanley shrugged.

"Thanks for coming down on such short notice," Anna said. She slid the file toward Stanley. "I didn't have anything on the sellers, other than what was in the contract. I gave you a printout from my contacts database on the sellers' attorney. It's got his address and phone number and email. I checked on the Internet. It's all current. Ditto their accountant. They're both Bahamian. If they have stateside offices, I couldn't find them. You also asked about their banker. I didn't have that, but I gave you the name and address of the bank. Likewise Bahamian. Best I could do. Hope that helps. What's this for, if you don't mind my asking?"

"It's a long story." Stanley cleared his throat. "Turns out Pete was trying to put together a group of investors to buy Homebase and hire him to run it. One of them contacted me a couple of days ago. Pete was apparently writing them an analysis of the website. Something more, how shall I put this, informative than whatever they'd read in the auctioneer's bid package."

Anna clicked her ballpoint pen open, made a check on her legal pad, and clicked the pen shut. "That's one of the topics on my agenda. The bid package, I mean. Why did they contact you?"

"They hired us to find it. Pete's analysis. Or his notes, anyway."

Anna glanced at Dave, who was somnambulant and drooling.

"Well, I hope you found it."

"No luck. I spent the morning over in Bensenville going through the Homebase files, but there's precious little there. In particular, nothing showing how to get in touch with the sellers. Which is why I asked for this." Stanley put his hand on the file.

"Well, if you call their attorney, don't be surprised to learn they fired him." She leaned forward, resting her hands on her elbows, and scowled. "He accepted our contract and closing documents without asking for a single change. I mean, not one."

Stanley nodded. "I noticed there wasn't much in the way of draft documents."

"If we were dealing with an attorney from Chicago or New York, we'd have a stack of drafts this high," Anna said, raising her hand above her head. "This attorney the sellers hired was nice enough, but if you want my opinion, he was way out of his league."

Stanley pursed his lips. "For ten million dollars you'd think they'd be more careful."

Anna shrugged. "Maybe they didn't care. They were, after all, on the receiving end of the money. Still, there were representations and warranties in there that I would have never let you sign." She waved her hand. "But that's history. So these investors. Why do they want to track down the sellers?"

"They want to talk to them about Homebase. To get a leg up on the other bidders." Stanley leaned forward. "Is that kosher, Anna? Can I help them do that?"

"What? Put a group of prospective Homebase purchasers in touch with the people you bought it from? Why not? Your duty's to the creditors, not the bidders."

"That's a relief. I was just concerned that it would seem wrong. Especially because I have a personal interest in it. Beyond the money I'll pocket from the sale."

"What's that?"

"They want me to run Homebase if they buy it."

"Good for you. Then I hope they do buy it. For your sake." Anna took a drink of water and clicked open her pen. "Now. Speaking of Mr. Tilden. He was also working on a narrative about Homebase for the auctioneer's bid package. We should have had it weeks ago. He kept promising . . ." She shook her head, her blond hair sweeping her shoulders. "And now we've got a major time crunch. I mean, we really need to print the bid package. So, you think you can write the narrative?"

"Me?" Stanley asked. "Frankly, Anna, I can't tell you much more about Homebase than its name. That, and in retrospect we were stupid to buy it."

"Well, you could summarize the key contracts. How's that?"

Stanley shrugged. "You want to give them to me, I'll go through them and do the best I can. But isn't that the trustee's job?"

Anna looked down at the legal pad. She started to make a note, then clicked her pen rapid-fire. Without looking at Stanley she said, "Are you saying you don't have copies of the contracts?"

"Never did, Anna. Why?"

Anna tapped the pen on the pad, scowling. Then she looked up at Stanley and said pointedly, "This is bad."

"What's bad, Anna?"

"Nobody seems to have any of the Homebase contracts. I know we don't. The trustee insists he's never seen them. Everybody was banking on you."

"What are you talking about, Anna?"

Anna drew a big zero on the legal pad. "Just what I said. No contracts."

"But what about from the purchase?" Stanley asked. "The due diligence? You would have gotten copies then."

"All we have are the purchase agreement and the closing

documents. Mr. Tilden handled the due diligence himself."

"But what about new advertising contracts? And all the operational stuff? Agreements with the web host? Weren't you working with Pete on those?"

"Mr. Tilden never hired us to do anything after the closing," she said, drawing geometric doodles on the pad. "We just assumed that you never went beyond the contracts you bought." She cleared her throat. "That or you were having them reviewed by another attorney."

Stanley shook his head. "Pete would have told me. And you say the trustee doesn't have them either?"

Anna spread her hands and shrugged her shoulders.

The significance of the information suddenly erupted in Stanley's head like the blast of a volcano come to life. He grabbed the edge of the table to steady himself, and asked, softly but in a tone so edged with concern that the words sounded metallic, like a trumpet, "Anna, is anybody running Homebase now?"

Anna clicked her pen several times before answering. "We were hoping you were."

"What about Pete's old Jamos Company staff? They might know something."

"We called everyone," Anna said. "But none of them said they had anything to do with Homebase." She drew a big circle around her doodles. "They offered—"

"Anna," Stanley interrupted, even more softly. "Does anybody even know how to run it?"

Anna tossed the pen on the legal pad and crossed her arms and looked Stanley in the eyes. "If anybody does, Mr. Jamos, I can't tell you who it would be."

Stanley rubbed his temples. "So let me see if I got this right. The contracts we bought with the website. The advertising. Everything else. The only person who had them was Pete?"

"Best as we can tell."

"And they're not in Bensenville. Which means they must be at Pete's house." Stanley shook his head with astonishment. "What I can't understand is how the trustee could have let this happen. I mean, wasn't it his job to keep Homebase running until the auction?"

"Technically. But since Mr. Tilden was the most qualified person . . . And it never occurred to anyone that he'd be . . ."

Stanley stared at Anna over the rims of his bifocals. "People die from other causes, Anna. They get in automobile accidents. They get sick."

"Look, I'm not trying to be the trustee's apologist. He should have had backup, no question about it." Anna took a deep breath, grabbed the glass and turned it slowly, staring at the ice cubes. "But it's more than that. The trustee's been asking Mr. Tilden for the Homebase contracts since the case was converted to Chapter Seven. And the auctioneer's been hounding him for a description for the bid package. And Mr. Tilden kept promising . . ."

Stanley waited for Anna to finish her comment. When he realized she had, he said, "I think I get the picture. Can we get them from Pete's house?"

"It's still a crime scene. We'll need a court order, unless the police agree to cooperate."

"Then get the trustee over to the police to ask."

Anna grabbed her pen, clicked it open and jotted something on the legal pad. "There's a little problem," she said. "The trustee's on vacation all week. Scuba diving in Bonaire or someplace. I tried calling him but no cell phone service. And God forbid there's some technical problem . . ."

"Isn't there someone else in the trustee's office?"

Anna shook her head. "They all work for themselves. Nobody there'll touch it."

After a painful silence, Stanley asked, "So what do we do?"

"You probably have the best shot at getting the police to release the Homebase files."

"Anna," Stanley said, "the police treat me like I'm a suspect in the murder."

Anna waved her hand dismissively. "Oh, they treat everyone that way."

"And if they won't?"

"Then we petition the court. But that takes time."

Stanley started to rise. "Well, at least we agree on one thing."

"And that is?"

"This is bad." He picked up the file, nudged Dave and said, "Let's go."

As they walked out of the conference room Anna paused and cleared her throat. "Let me ask you something, Mr. Jamos. What was your reason for buying Homebase?"

"Didn't Pete explain it? We could bundle our marketing business with direct access to Gen Y consumers."

"No, what I meant was, why buy? Why not license?"

"I never thought about it, really," Stanley confessed. "I guess I just left it up to Pete to make the right call."

Anna took another sip of water. "I realize your circumstances weren't typical, but even so, companies just don't diversify as part of a strategy to be acquired. Divest, if anything. A license from Homebase would have made more sense. You would still have access to their user base for a heck of a lot cheaper. Anyway, that was what I recommended to Mr. Tilden."

"He never mentioned it to me. What did he say?"

Another pause. Another clearing of the throat. "Mr. Tilden said the price was too good an opportunity to pass up."

"What did you think of the price, Anna?"

"I'm not qualified . . ."

Stanley put his hand on Anna's shoulder. "I'm not asking for a legal opinion. Just your personal assessment. Based on your experience."

"Ten million was a steal, for what it was represented to be. But that still didn't make it consistent with your goal of finding a buyer for Jamos Company. Any more than buying an under-priced Rembrandt would have."

"Why didn't you discuss the license directly with me?"

"Well . . ."

"Was it because of my Parkinson's? Did you think I wasn't competent to deal with it?"

"Mr. Jamos," Anna protested. "I'm quite familiar with the disease. My mother-in-law has it. Competence was hardly an issue."

"Did Pete tell you not to discuss it with me?"

"Certainly not. And if he had, he knew perfectly well, and I hope you do too, it would have been an instruction I would have been ethically obligated to ignore. I would have told him so myself."

"Well, what then?"

"Nothing sinister, Mr. Jamos. Mr. Tilden told me you'd delegated the Homebase project to him. You and Mr. Mosit signed shareholders' and directors' resolutions approving the purchase and loan and authorizing Mr. Tilden to sign the neces-sary documents. And we did talk about the loan documents. Remember? So it was pretty clear you were okay with the acquisition. No, he never told us not to talk to you. He just said not to bother you with the details unless we thought it was necessary. But since the sellers accepted our contract one hundred percent, there weren't really any details to discuss." Another cough. Another clearing of the throat. Another sip of water.

"Is that it, Anna? Or is there more?"

The elevator chimed and the door opened. Anna wedged her

foot in to keep it from closing. "You're going to think I'm blowing things out of proportion."

"Right about now," Stanley said, "that would be pretty hard to do."

"It just crossed my mind. Whoever robbed Mr. Tilden—robbed and killed him—maybe that's what they were looking for? The Homebase files?"

CHAPTER 17

When Stanley asked the day clerk for Detectives Birkholz and Hustad, he expected to be taken to their desks. Instead, he and Dave were shown into what was obviously an interrogation room and told to sit at the far end of the table. A camera mounted on the opposite wall was aimed at them. The LED beneath the lens wasn't lit, but Stanley didn't assume that meant the camera was off.

A few minutes passed before the detectives entered. Birkholz sat under the camera. Hustad stood by the door, his droopy eyes darting between Stanley and Dave.

Birkholz casually ran his fingers across the gouges in the desk. Stanley could envision suspects clawing at the laminate with their fingernails as cops worked them over. The room had the stale aroma of tobacco and coffee and human fluids secreted under duress.

Birkholz gestured with his thumb at Dave's hat and asked Stanley, "He ever take that off?" He held up a hand to stop Stanley from answering. "None of my business one way or the other. So what can we do for you gentlemen?"

"Well," Stanley began amiably, "Pete ran a Jamos Company subsidiary named Homebase. Seems he had all the business records at his house. I was hoping . . ."

Birkholz twisted his mustache. "You're not here to tell us about Ed Lind?"

Stanley sighed. "I told you. I never met the man."

"Then how come he has Jamos Company holiday cards in his office? Personally signed by you?"

"Not by me," Stanley said. "My secretary, probably."

"You can prove that?"

Stanley extended his left hand, palm down. It quivered. "I can prove I didn't sign one in the last four years."

Birkholz stared at the shaking hand for a moment, then said, "Convenient. But it doesn't explain your new office."

"What about my new office?" Stanley asked, endeavoring to suppress his annoyance.

"Your landlord."

"What about my landlord?"

Birkholz lit a cigarette and leaned forward. "Don't play coy with me. You know perfectly well where your rent goes."

Stanley looked at Hustad for a clue, but Hustad was examining his fingernails. Stanley looked back at Birkholz. "Metropolitan Rental Agency?"

Birkholz tugged gently at the tip of his mustache. "Not that. The owner of the building."

Stanley spread his hands, exasperated. "That's all I know."

"You saying you have no idea?" Hustad asked.

Stanley shook his head.

"Then let us educate you," Birkholz said with feigned patience. "It's owned by a land trust. The beneficiary of which is none other than our old friend, Jefferson and Maxwell Office Supplies, Incorporated. Which in turn is owned by Ed Lind. Who you say you never met." Birkholz interlocked his fingers and spun his thumbs in circles around each other. "Does that, as my lawyer friends like to say, refresh your memory?"

"Officer," Stanley said, sounding to himself like he was pleading, "I have no idea who this Lind person is."

"Things are starting to unravel, Mr. Jamos," Birkholz said. "You're running out of time to come clean."

179

"Maybe there's an innocent explanation?" Hustad offered. "I mean, if you found the space through a broker who can confirm it's just a coincidence . . ."

"We didn't use a broker," Stanley said. "Pete told me to check it out."

"Pete as in Mr. Tilden?"

Stanley nodded.

"So let me see if I got this straight. You just"—Birkholz formed quotation marks with his fingers—"happen to be renting your office from Ed Lind's company. And the person who"—Birkholz again formed quotation marks with his fingers—"happened to set you up there just happens to be the victim. Isn't everything so convenient." His eyes bore into Stanley's.

"Look," Stanley pleaded. "Will you just hear me out on why I came here?"

"We're all ears," Birkholz said.

Stanley cleared his throat and took a deep breath to regain as much composure as possible before beginning. "Jamos Company has a subsidiary called Homebase. Pete ran it from his house. There must have been boxes and boxes of contracts and documents. I'm going to have to take over control of it. I was hoping you could help me get them."

"Well, gee," Birkholz said, "why don't you just ask us?"

"You mean it? Really?" Stanley asked, relieved.

"No," Birkholz said pointedly, "I most certainly do not. This is a murder investigation, Mr. Jamos. Everything in Mr. Tilden's house is presumed to be evidence. Even your"—he made quotation marks with his fingers—" 'boxes and boxes.' "

"But these files don't belong to Pete," Stanley protested. "They belong to the company."

"That makes them yours, does it?" Birkholz asked.

"Technically . . ."

" 'Technically'? That's lawyer talk. My job is to solve a murder, Mr. Jamos. Not your technical problems."

"Would it help if I have my lawyer call you?"

"Your lawyer happen to know who killed Mr. Tilden?"

"No," Stanley said. "I meant . . ."

"I know exactly what you meant," Birkholz said, punctuating his annoyance with an angry wave of his hand. "Besides, I am *so* afraid of lawyers." He thrust out his hand and shook it. "See how I'm trembling?"

Fury seethed in Stanley. He stood and said, "Come on, Dave. We're out of here."

"Mr. Jamos," Hustad said gently. "We can't help you."

"Yeah," Stanley said, struggling to get his arms through the sleeves of his overcoat. "I'm beginning to figure that out."

"I don't mean we won't," Hustad said, helping Stanley with his overcoat. "I mean we can't. There weren't any boxes of anything that looked like business records. Or unboxed records, for that matter."

This is bad, Stanley thought. He slumped back onto the chair. "That's impossible."

"These documents," Hustad asked. "How important were they?"

"They were invaluable."

"Who stood to benefit from them?"

"Ultimately, the three of us. Dave," he said, nodding toward Dave who was putting on his coat, "Pete and me."

Hustad crossed his arms. "Let's look at it from another angle. Who stood to benefit if they disappeared?"

Stanley remembered Anna's parting question. It seemed less implausible. "Only Homebase's competitors," Stanley said. "The website would be real precarious until the records are reconstructed. If they're not found, it could collapse." He realized there was another angle. "There's something else. The website's being auctioned in two months. And if the auctioneer doesn't have the records, nobody will bid on it. So whoever has them could pick it up for a song."

"What's it worth?"

"We paid ten million for it."

Hustad whistled. "Ten million doesn't sound like a song to me."

"Except it's real similar to other websites that sold for hundreds of millions."

Hustad looked at Birkholz. "You thinking what I'm thinking?"

Birkholz crushed out his cigarette on the surface of the table. "Motive," he said.

Before pulling out from the police station parking lot, Stanley called Ronnie. Phone wedged between his ear and his shoulder, he leafed through the file Anna had given him. "Let's see. Letter from the attorney, with address, phone, fax, and email. Email from the accountant, same information. Name and address of the sellers' bank, but no contact." He closed the file. "Nothing on the sellers. You want me to start with the attorney?" He put the file on the dashboard.

"Oh, my God, no!" Ronnie said hastily. "He'll just assume you're calling to accuse his clients of breaching the contract and won't take the call."

"The accountant, then?"

"Let me think." After a brief silence, Ronnie said, "Tell you what. Drop it off and I'll send it to my boys. They have connections. They'll figure out someone who knows the lawyer or the accountant or one of the bank's directors. They'll grease the path for you, so you won't be hung up on when you call."

"Sounds good to me," Stanley said.

Stanley swung by the hotel. Ronnie was standing outside,

smoking a cigarette and stomping her feet to stay warm. She waved at Stanley and made a circular gesture with her hand for him to roll down the passenger-side window.

"Hi, Dave," she said. She leaned in and kissed Dave on the cheek.

"Do I know you?" Dave asked.

She stroked his cheek. "You did. A long time ago."

Stanley placed the file in her outstretched hand. "Dinner?" he asked

"Can't tonight. Another deal I thought I was finished with just went haywire." She turned and began to walk back to the hotel.

"Sure," Stanley said. He sensed a frigidity in the air unrelated to the March weather. *Why not?* he thought. *Last night was the second time I blew you off.* "See you tomorrow at the funeral," he said to her back.

If Ronnie heard him, she didn't acknowledge it.

Stanley pulled out and turned north on State Street. Through the rearview mirror he watched Ronnie, the file jammed in her arm, stub out her cigarette before entering the hotel.

★ ★ ★ ★ ★

THURSDAY

★ ★ ★ ★ ★

CHAPTER 18

The funeral was in Blue Island, on Chicago's far south, the last place Stanley would have expected a service for a north-sider like Pete. Snow was falling hard enough to cover the footprints of mourners who'd already arrived.

A snow shovel leaned against one of the ionic columns supporting the portico. Stanley pointed at it and said to Mary, "Must be decorative."

When Stanley entered the building, an enormous white angel statue stared back at him with haunting, painted eyes. Its wings were chipped. What had looked from the outside to be stained glass windows were, Stanley observed, sheets of plastic affixed to the foyer windows by masking tape. The paint was splotched and peeling, the carpets worn and the foyer's broken radiator clanked futilely.

Stanley pushed open the door to the anteroom. The four men and two women already there turned in unison and abruptly stopped talking. Practically gasping, they nodded uncomfortably at Stanley and hurriedly resumed artificially animated conversations.

Mary stepped in front of Stanley and feigned brushing his overcoat lapels so that she could get close enough to whisper, "Someone here doesn't like you."

The chapel doors were closed. Stanley signaled with his eyes in the direction of the door leading back to the foyer. Carrying her overcoat over her arm, she followed him out.

"Pete's staff," Stanley explained. "It's the first time we've seen each other since the judge released them from their non-competes and they jumped ship." He frowned. "I knew they'd be here. Woke up in the middle of the night worrying about how I'd take seeing them."

"Was it uncomfortable for you?"

"For me?" Stanley laughed. "You see the way they squirmed when I walked in?"

The front door opened. Dave entered in a swirl of snow, as if blown there by the wind. Cindy followed.

"Mary, this is my partner Dave I've been telling you about," Stanley said. "And his wife, Cindy. Dave, Cindy, I'd like you to meet Mary Sullivan."

"I am so sorry for your loss," Mary said to Dave. "I just wish we could have met under better circumstances." She extended a hand.

Dave shook it hesitantly. "Do I know you?" he asked.

"No, but I've heard so much about you from Stanley." She turned to Cindy and gave her a consoling hug.

Dave looked around the room and asked, "Where's Pete?"

Stanley nodded toward the door to the anteroom. "In there."

"Can I talk to him?"

The front door opened again. Nick entered, brushing snow off his coat. "Well, well!" he said. He gave Cindy a hug with one arm while he reached up and tried to remove Dave's hat with the other. Dave dodged the effort with surprising agility. Nick turned to Mary. "Mary, isn't it?"

"Hi, Nick," Mary said.

"Drinks at my place after sundown," Nick announced as he removed his overcoat. "We're going to send Pete off in style."

The door to the anteroom swung open, pushed by a beefy man with a graying crewcut wearing a black polyester suit and black leather running shoes. A laminated card pinned to his

lapel read, FUNERAL HOME DIRECTOR. "Tilden funeral?"
he asked.

"That's us," Nick said.

The man glanced at his wristwatch. "Better go in and pay
your respects, folks. We got another starting in less than an
hour."

Nick was first to the casket. He leaned over, stared at Pete's
body, whispered a few inaudible words, stood and said, "Love
you, man." He turned and stepped aside to make room for
Stanley and Mary.

Stanley looked down.

On his back, eyes closed, hands clasped, Pete looked asleep,
so much so that the stark absence of motion seemed the illusion. The mouth was taut, the ends tilted up in an expression
he'd never displayed in life. The cosmetologist had compensated
for the cause of death by sweeping bangs over his forehead.

Stanley fought the urge to reach in and brush the hair away.
He expected that the bullet hole would be caulked and painted
over, but felt tugged by a delicious thrill at the thought of
uncovering a gaping wound, an artificial third eye staring at the
eternal emptiness. It made him want to giggle. He stepped back.

Mary dropped on one knee before the casket and crossed
herself.

The front row of seats was cordoned by a sign that read
RESERVED FOR FAMILY. Only two were occupied, by a man
roughly Stanley's age who Stanley didn't recognize and a
chubby woman many years his junior. The man's thin brown
hair was carefully combed across his scalp and sealed in place
with something dark and oily. His suit was ill-fitting but
elegantly tailored. His companion wore her bleached hair in a
pageboy and makeup so thick it creased in places, lining her
face with unnatural wrinkles. An armory of gold and large stones
hung from her neck, wrists, and fingers. The man held his hat in

his hands. He was speaking to Nick, who was standing in front of him, but seemed to be addressing Nick's chest.

"Hey," Nick said to Stanley. "You two know each other?"

The man had the sort of face and expression that made Stanley think he ought to know him from somewhere. Not recently, but from some context that had long since ceased to have relevance in Stanley's life. Stanley extended his hand and said, "Do we? You do look familiar."

The man shook Stanley's hand and said, looking at it rather than Stanley as if it were something requiring closer examination, "I don't think so. Ed Lind."

Stanley's jaw dropped. "*You're* Ed Lind?"

"And this is my bride, Nancy," Ed said, placing his hand with conspicuous pride on his companion's pudgy shoulder. The woman reached up and put her hand on Ed's, bracelets spilling and tinkling down her wrist. "Didn't catch yours."

"Stanley," Stanley said. "Jamos."

"Well, what do you know? Stanley Jamos, in the flesh," Ed said to Stanley's chest. "Damn! Excuse my French. And after all these years."

"Eddie's Pete's cousin," Nick explained.

Mary leaned forward. "Hi," she said. "I'm Mary Sullivan."

"Nice to meet you," Ed told Mary's shoes.

"You from around here?" Stanley asked.

"Nearby," Ed nodded. "Beverly. Real shame about your company. Lost my biggest account."

"A blessing in disguise, if you ask me," Nancy interjected. "Forced him into early retirement." She gripped Ed's arm in hers and smiled at Stanley with a mouth caked in bright red lipstick. "Best thing that ever happened to him. Used to be off on sales calls weeks at a time. Now we travel together everywhere. In fact, Eddie surprised me this morning. He's taking me to the Bahamas on Sunday." She looked lovingly at Ed and squeezed his arm. "What about you, Mr. Jamos? Do you travel much?"

"Not so much," Stanley said, "these days."

In the periphery of his vision Stanley caught a motion. A priest, looking nervous, entered from a door to the right of the casket, furtively tucking note cards into a fold of his robe.

"Had to rent the priest," Ed whispered to Stanley and Nick. "Pete didn't believe in the stuff. If he knew I was throwing him a funeral he'd have a fit."

"Eddie!" Nancy chastised.

Stanley scanned the room. Pete's staff were sitting in the fourth row, to the left of the center aisle. Dave and Cindy were in the second row, to the right, behind Ed and Nancy. The rest of the chairs were unoccupied.

Ronnie wasn't there.

As he sat he wondered, *Did she even know where to go?* He tapped Ed on the shoulder and asked, "Did Ronnie Dumat call you for directions?"

"Who?" Ed replied.

The priest coughed and began a dignified shuffle to the pulpit. He ran a hand across his bald head and cleared his throat. "We gather today to mourn the loss of our dear friend Peter Roy Tilden. But though we grieve, let our hearts sing with gladness. Because he left this world for a far better place, where he will spend eternity in the loving grace of Our Lord and Shepherd."

Stanley was suddenly overcome with fatigue from the meds. The priest's words droned like the buzzing of insects on a muggy summer night. A few times Mary elbowed him when the congregants were expected to sing, to stand, to kneel, but he ignored her. A pause in the service caused him to open his eyes.

The priest was fumbling awkwardly through the note cards, trying to assemble a eulogy. He looked at one, put it down, looked at the next, turned it around. "I didn't have the privilege of knowing Peter . . . Pete . . . His friends called him Pete." The priest paused, coughed, dropped the card, stooped to pick it up. For an agonizing moment Stanley thought that was all he had to say.

"He was a solid citizen, a hard worker. Worked at the same company since he graduated from college, as a . . ." He turned a card over. "Technology specialist. He never had children of his own, but his friends describe him as warm to their children, and . . ." The priest paused and stared at another card. "And he was very religious, too. A strong moral fiber. His friends said he was a man who knew right from wrong and always stood up for . . ." The priest coughed again. "What was right. A decent, hard-working man."

"Good thing he's dead," Stanley whispered to Mary, "because this guy's killing him."

"Shh!"

"Does anyone have memories of Pete to share with us?" The priest spread his arms, beckoning. "Please come up," he pleaded, sounding desperate.

The seconds paraded past, punctuated by the sounds of shuffling feet and nervous coughs.

The funeral home director, who had been standing to the side, hands clasped behind his back and head solemnly down during the service, glanced at his wristwatch and frowned. He strode quickly to the podium and edged the priest away. The priest shrank back, almost stumbling, and seemed to deflate. "I've been asked to announce," the director bellowed, "that I have a list of worthy causes for donations in the deceased's memory." He held up a small paper. "If you're interested, please come see me. And now, if you'll all please exit through the door on your right."

"When I die," Mary said to Stanley as they rose, "would you

please make sure that the service is packed? Even if you have to pay people to attend?"

Stanley stood, turned and scanned the room again for Ronnie. *Where the hell is she?*

He tapped Ed Lind on the shoulder and said, "Look. I realize this really isn't the time or place to ask, but I have to know. Did the police question you about the murder?"

Ed stared uncomfortably at his shoes. "Boy, did they ever."

"Me, too," Stanley said. "They told me you said we knew each other. Did you tell them that?"

For a fleeting instant Ed looked Stanley directly in the eyes. Stanley noticed that Ed's right eye was gray, his left blue. "They told me the same thing. Only they said that's what you told them." Ed's eyes narrowed. He started to put on his overcoat. "I don't know what's going on, but I got the impression they got no leads and are looking for someone to frame."

As they walked out of the chapel, Mary asked, "So where's Ronnie?"

"I don't get it," Stanley said. "She wasn't here." He swung open the funeral home door and held it for Mary. Then he stepped into the daylight and immediately froze. "Oh, shit."

"What's wrong?" Mary asked.

Stanley said, "Wait here a minute." He left Mary and crossed the street to the dark sedan with the engine idling and tapped on the driver's window.

The tinted window rolled down. Birkholz looked up at Stanley. "Don't tell me we missed the funeral?"

Stanley started to speak but bit his lip, fearing all that would come out would be a stream of obscenities.

Birkholz exhaled smoke and pitched the cigarette butt out the window. It missed Stanley, but not by much. "You still sticking to your story that you never met Ed Lind?"

Stanley pivoted angrily and began to cross the street.

"Mr. Jamos?" Hustad's disembodied voice asked.

Stanley stopped and turned.

Hustad ducked to see and be visible to Stanley through Birkholz's window. "We mean no disrespect. But we still got loose ends. Parts of Mr. Lind's story don't add up."

Birkholz shifted the car into gear. "And if his story don't add up," he said, pulling away, "neither does yours."

CHAPTER 19

Tracy sat behind the register, reading the *Tribune*. She looked up as Stanley came through the door. It was evident she'd been crying.

Stanley helped himself to a doughnut and a cup of decaf.

"Late start?" Tracy asked. "I missed you at breakfast."

"Funeral."

"Sorry," Tracy said. "Relative?"

"Friend."

"Even worse. Where's Dave?"

"He was there too. His wife took him home."

"You want lunch?"

Stanley held up the doughnut and patted his stomach. "This'll do."

"Those two guys who've been eating here this week? Leather jackets? They were here this morning. Asked where you were."

"They say anything in particular?"

Tracy shrugged. "Just wanted to know if you'd come and gone." She reached for another tissue and loudly blew her nose.

Stanley squinted over his bifocals to get a better look at her. "You doing okay?"

She answered with a loud honk of her nose and dabbed away a tear. "That asshole? It just gets better and better. Seems Raul, the dishwasher, has a sister. Turns out that's who Jake's been banging. Raul knew all about it. Said 'Gracias' every time I gave him his check and smiled and never said a word about it to me." She choked on a sob. "Some kind of sick macho male bonding thing, I guess. And to make matters worse, now that Jake's leaving me for her, Raul figures he can't work here anymore. So in addition to being out one inheritance, one chef and one husband, I'm also out one dishwasher."

"Dishwashers shouldn't be that hard to find."

"Shows what you know about the restaurant business. And even if I could, how am I supposed to take people's orders and cook them up and clean the tables and wash the dishes in the meantime?"

Stanley shrugged. "So close down until you find a replacement."

"Yeah," Tracy muttered. "I'm sure the bank'll understand."

"Jingle Bells" squeaked through the tinny speaker. Two women walked in, hand in hand. Stanley guessed late twenties. The blonde was gaunt enough to be anorexic. Her buzz-cut companion wore a University of Illinois at Chicago sweatshirt and loose jeans.

Tracy walked around from the register, carrying two menus. "Sit anywhere," she invited.

The women opted for the counter. Buzz-cut studied Tracy. "Something wrong, honey?"

"Man trouble," Tracy said too quickly.

In unison, the women glared at Stanley.

"Hey!" Stanley said, holding up his hands to ward off their curse. "I'm not the man at issue."

The blonde put the menu down and asked Tracy, "How late do you serve breakfast?"

"Breakfast, lunch, dinner served 'round the clock," Tracy said.

"Great, because I've got a taste for pancakes."

"What's good here?" Buzz-cut asked.

"Everything," Tracy insisted.

"If you're in the mood for spicy," Stanley volunteered, "go for the *Chef Recommends* breakfast special. But don't count on quick service. The chef, also known as Tracy's husband, quit both jobs." He sensed they'd be sympathetic.

The blonde smiled at Tracy. "Then one pancakes and one special it is. And take your time, honey. Coffee when you can."

Buzz-cut turned to Stanley. "You from around here?"

"My office is next door," Stanley said.

"How's the neighborhood?"

Stanley shrugged. "Quiet. And cheap."

"There's a building a block west. Four story, brick."

"The one with the fire escape in front?"

Buzz-cut nodded. "We're thinking about opening a women's art collective. Studios, galleries, that sort of thing. Plus day care. What do you think? Is it safe?"

"Never had any problems," Stanley said. "Not much foot traffic, but that'll change. You can see the condos are moving this way."

"That's what we were thinking," she said. "Get in while the getting's good."

Stanley looked at his watch. "Time to get back," he said. "Hope it works out for you." As he passed Tracy at the cash register on his way out he whispered, "Buy Jake out as soon as you can. The artists are coming."

CHAPTER 20

Two human forms paused outside the frosted glass. One raised an arm and rapped, three crisp knocks.

"It's open," Stanley said.

Doug entered, hands stuffed in his jeans pockets, eyes darting about the office. Tim followed, shutting the door delicately, as if a slam would shatter the glass and send JAMOS & MOSIT, INC., PRIVATE INVESTIGATORS into oblivion.

Stanley put down the pen with which he'd been doing the crossword puzzle and pushed the *Tribune* to the side of the desk. "Well, hello," he said, starting to rise.

Tim waved at him to sit. "You busy?"

"Not at all," Stanley said. "Come in. Nice to see you."

"Didn't see you at the diner this morning," Tim said. He set his duffel bag on the floor and eased himself into the client seat. "Wanted to follow up on that job I was discussing with you the other day."

"Would have called," Doug said. "Couldn't get the number from information." He pushed Dave's chair next to Tim and sat.

Something in Doug's tone struck Stanley as accusatory. He held up his cell phone. "No land line," he said. His voice sounded weakly apologetic.

"That so?" Doug said. His gaze swept the office again, a process that didn't take long. Stanley had the disembodied sensation of seeing the office from Doug's perspective in all its paltriness. His mouth went dry.

"Where's your partner?" Tim asked.

"Took the day off. Funeral."

"Sorry to hear it," Tim said. "Where do your clients sit when he's here?"

"We've never had a client come here," Stanley said.

Tim nodded pensively. "Meet them at their place, do you?"

"At restaurants," Stanley said tentatively. "Mostly."

"Mostly?" Doug repeated.

"So this is where you do your work, then?" Tim asked.

Stanley nodded. "How can I help you?"

"You remember the job?"

"You mean the guy who sold you some hot jewelry?"

Tim nodded. "You think you can handle it?"

"I . . ." Stanley began. He didn't know how to conclude the sentence.

"What?" Tim asked. "Not your line of work? Or just too busy with other stuff?"

Stanley stammered. He couldn't make sense out of the syllables he heard himself speak. He had no idea what he was trying to say.

Tim glanced at Doug.

Doug said, "This is too painful," and nodded.

Tim took a deep breath. "Look, let's not beat around the bush, okay? I really like you. But this . . ." His hand swept a circle, taking in the room. "No telephones. No file cabinets. I mean, come on."

"What are you saying?"

"You're not a detective, are you?" Doug asked. His tone was gentle, sympathetic.

And suddenly Stanley understood. "Who *are* you guys?"

"From your insurance company, Mr. Jamos." Doug unzipped the duffel bag, reached in and pulled out a card. He gave it to

Tim, who leaned forward to hand it to Stanley. "Insurance fraud."

Stanley stared at the card. All the words blurred except INVESTIGATOR, which stood out like BRIDGE OUT AHEAD or DANGER FALLING ROCKS.

"Didn't you think a detective agency where the owners are filing claims for diseases like Alzheimer's and Parkinson's would wave a red flag?" Doug asked.

"The computer spat out your file," Tim said. "We got sent to investigate."

"Nothing personal," Doug added.

Tim spread his hands. "We just file a report. We don't make recommendations. If you don't like the outcome, you can challenge it."

"What will the report say?" Stanley asked, his desiccated tongue crackling the words.

"That we paid you a visit at the office address listed on the application. That you occupied said office. That we found no indication of business being conducted."

"And then what happens?"

"My guess?" Tim shrugged. "You'll be given two options. Immediate cancellation with reimbursement waived. Which I'm required to advise you will screw up continuity of coverage. Or premium adjustment to the level of a non-corporate policy, both retroactive and prospective, until you find another insurer. But no renewal when the policy expires." He stood. "Look, we're just the messengers here. If it were up to me, I'd let sleeping dogs lie. But the bean counters get paid by the cancellation. Bunch of assholes, but that's who signs our checks."

"I'm sorry, Mr. Jamos," Doug said. "Like I said. It's nothing personal. I'm with Tim. If it were my decision to make . . ." He shrugged apologetically.

"Blame it on the computer," Tim said.

"But we really are working a case," Stanley said. His voice was so hoarse he had to clear his throat twice.

"Look, you got something to prove you're legit, we'll be happy to put it in our report."

"Like what?"

"You know. Retainer agreements, tax returns, copies of checks, bank statements. Anything that shows you're in business."

"I don't . . . have anything here," Stanley said. "I can call my bank and get you a copy of a recent deposit . . ."

"We can sit on this for a couple of days," Tim said. "You got something for us, give me a call and we'll send it in with the report."

At the door, Doug paused, turned around and added, "If you really are in the investigation business, or decide to get in, a tip. Don't trust nobody. And that includes your clients."

Stanley stared at the door for nearly a minute after they left. Then he called his insurance agent.

He got an answering machine.

He left a message.

Stanley's cell phone launched into "Surfin' USA." "Yeah," Stanley answered, expecting the insurance agent.

"Stanley Jamos or David Mosit, please." The voice lacked the cheeriness of a sales call. To the contrary, it had the timbre of a messenger with bad news.

"This is Stanley."

"Mr. Jamos? I'm with your bank. Two days ago you made a five-thousand-dollar deposit?"

"Yes?" Stanley said. But he knew what he'd hear.

"I'm sorry, but the issuer stopped payment."

Stanley was relieved. He thought he was going to be told it had been rejected for insufficient funds.

He called Ronnie's hotel. He was told that Ms. Dumat had checked out last night.

"Surfin' USA" again. Stanley looked at the caller ID but didn't recognize the number. "Yes?" he asked cautiously.

"Mr. Jamos? Detective Hustad, Eighteenth District. We checked with Mr. Tilden's housekeeper. About those boxes of business records you mentioned."

"Yes?"

"I think I have good news for you."

"I could use some good news," Stanley said.

"We can rule out their being stolen during the murder. She doesn't remember ever seeing any boxes of that description in Mr. Tilden's house."

CHAPTER 21

Nick had the neon CLOSED sign turned on. "I close up whenever he brings good-looking women around," he explained to Mary.

"And how often is that?" Mary asked. She jammed two quarters in the jukebox and punched the number for Chuck Berry's "Too Much Monkey Business."

"You're the first."

"Come on," she said to Stanley, arms above her head, fingers snapping. "Dance with me."

"I don't know how to dance," Stanley protested.

"So stand next to me and shake," she said. "You ought to be pretty good at that." She winked at Nick.

"I do so love Parkinson's jokes," Stanley groused.

Mary twirled over to Nick. "He was in a foul mood the whole ride over. Better break out the good stuff."

"What's bugging you, man?" Nick asked Stanley. To Mary, he asked, "You like bourbon?"

"Love it."

Nick draped an arm around her waist and steered her toward the bar. "If you like bourbon, darling, have I got a treat for you." Looking over his shoulder at Stanley, he added, "My pappy used to say, 'Son, you find a woman who appreciates a good bourbon, you marry her.'"

"So marry her," Stanley muttered. "Besides, you never had a

father. And in answer to your question, I had myself a shitty day."

"Sorry to hear it," Nick said. He produced a mason jar filled with a clear liquid and set it on the bar before Mary. "Check the label," he said proudly.

Mary rotated the jar. "There isn't one."

"Exactly. Official government un-regulated. The real deal." He unscrewed the lid and poured three glasses. "If you're a connoisseur you'll inhale the aroma first, then take a drop on the tongue, then sip it slowly." He tilted his head back, poured the liquid in his mouth, swallowed and slammed the glass on the bar. "If you're Irish? Down the hatch."

"Does part Scottish count?" Mary asked.

"It does at Nick's, darling."

"Then down the hatch," Mary said, tossing back the shot.

Nick turned to Stanley. "Care to join us?"

Stanley scowled, picked up his glass and turned away.

Nick winked at Mary. "Maybe if we ignore him, he'll leave."

Mary licked her lips. "What is this stuff?"

"Genuine corn liquor from the hills of Kentucky," Nick said, pouring seconds for himself and Mary.

"You mean moonshine?"

"The same. Ready?"

She nodded with mock solemnity. "Ready."

They touched glasses, said, "Down the hatch," and tossed back round two.

Mary licked her lips again. "That is so delicious."

Nick refilled their glasses. He raised his. "To our dear departed comrade Pete Tilden. Pete, I don't know where you are, but if you don't see the devil soon, you definitely took the wrong bus."

"To Pete," Stanley toasted unenthusiastically.

Mary said, "He must have been a hell of a guy to have you as friends. Sorry I never met him."

"A hell of a guy," Nick repeated. "That he was." He poured another round and raised his glass. "And now, if you'll excuse the indulgence. A toast to me."

"To you?" Stanley asked. "This better be good."

"It is, my friend." Nick cleared his throat and loosened the collar of the cowboy shirt he'd worn to the funeral, black with red roses embroidered on the breast pockets. "I made up my mind. I accepted an offer. I'm selling the place." He hopped up onto a bar stool. "I've been thinking about it for a while, but Pete's death put it all in perspective. It's been damned near forty years. Time for a change. Down the hatch, folks."

"Can I put in a bid on the jukebox?" Mary asked.

"Run off with me and you can have it."

"What'll you do?" Stanley asked.

Nick shrugged. "Travel. Read. Lead a normal life, maybe."

"I can imagine your devoted clientele will be devastated by the news," Stanley said.

"Go deal with the food, would you?" Nick asked Stanley. "It's in the cooler."

Mary looked from Nick to Stanley. "Am I missing something?"

"Tell her about your clientele, Nick."

"You're doing such a good job, you tell her."

"He bought this place after the Martin Luther King riots turned the whole area into a no man's land," Stanley explained to Mary. "Pinned between the Latin Kings, the P Stone Rangers, and a couple of others."

"They never bothered me," Nick said.

"I told him he was crazy. What amazes me," he said to Nick, "is how you stayed in business all this time."

"And which one of us went bankrupt?" Nick retorted. He turned to Mary and said, "Moneybags here thinks just because he came from a family with the scratch to buy a bar on Rush Street, so did everyone else."

"So he took a bar in the middle of nowhere that nobody in his right mind would walk in, and turns it into . . . Well, go ahead, Nick? What would you call it?"

"A bar, is what I'd call it."

"A bar whose only customers are what we used to call 'working girls.' Hold that thought." Stanley opened the latch on the cooler door, stepped in and emerged with a large round tray wrapped in cellophane.

"What's he talking about?" Mary asked Nick. "Prostitutes?"

Nick held up a hand to explain. "They'd come here with their tricks and the place would be so deserted they realized they could slip into a booth and . . . you know. Turned out to work quite nicely for them. Beat the alley. Cheaper than a hotel room. So they asked me if I could accommodate their business. They basically paid me to cut back on the lighting, take out some tables, install more booths, go easy on the decor. A mutually beneficial proposition. For lack of a better word."

"Are you kidding me?" Mary asked.

"It's the truth," Stanley said.

"I don't think of myself as a prude," Mary said. "But I have to say, I don't approve."

"What do you say to that, Nick?" Stanley asked as he set the tray on the bar and ripped into the plastic. "She doesn't approve. Where's the bagels? The pumpernickel?"

"Right here," Nick said, hoisting bags of bagels and black bread and paper plates and plastic utensils from under the counter. "And to you, ma'am, I say, doesn't matter. What's past is past. I'm out of here."

"What is all that?" Mary asked, staring at the tray.

"Lox," Stanley said, pointing at each item. "Smoked whitefish. Marinated herring. Tuna salad. Cream cheese."

"Shiva food," Nick added. "It's what Jews eat when someone dies."

"Pete was Jewish?"

"Jewish, Irish, what's the difference?" Nick said. "Point is, the living got to eat. And after a funeral, nothing beats Shiva food."

"Right," Stanley said. "The food of death. Got so much cholesterol, it speeds up the reunion with the deceased."

"Amen to that, brother," Nick said.

"And right about now I'd welcome a coronary."

"Just how bad a day *did* you have?" Nick asked.

"Bad," Stanley said.

Someone banged on the door. From outside Cindy called, "Anyone in there?"

"I'll get it," Stanley said. He opened the door.

"It's freezing out there," Cindy said, shivering, as she unbuttoned her coat.

Stanley put his hand on Dave's back and gave him a gentle shove in the direction of the bar. "Dave, get Nick to fix you something. Cindy, can I have a word? We have sort of a problem with our insurance." He led Cindy to a corner of the room.

Dave walked to the bar, put his fingers on a stool and gave it a spin.

"Take off your hat, pal," Nick said, reaching for the fedora. "This is a wake." Dave deftly dodged Nick's hand. Nick shrugged, pointed at the tray and handed Dave a paper plate. "Help yourself."

Dave picked up a bagel. Nibbling, he asked, "Who died?"

Cindy walked over to the bar, frowning, and said, "Give me a double."

"Say 'please,' " Nick said.

"Just give her the damned drink," Stanley muttered.

Nick looked at Cindy, then at Stanley, said, "Whatever," filled a large glass with moonshine and handed it to Cindy. She tilted it back and swallowed a third of it.

"I still don't follow," Cindy said to Stanley's reflection in the mirror. "Are you saying our insurance was or wasn't cancelled?"

"Cancelled at the current rate. We can keep it for the rest of the year if we pay the new rate, but they won't renew it."

"So what do we do?" Cindy downed the rest of her drink and held the glass out to Nick for a refill.

"We find new coverage, I guess," Stanley said. "I called our broker. He hasn't called back."

Cindy took another sip as soon as Nick finished pouring.

"Something wrong?" Mary asked Stanley.

"You could say that," Stanley said. He walked around the bar, got a beer stein and held it under the draft spigot. "You want to know how bad my day was? Pete's funeral was the high point. That's how bad." He took a swig of beer, picked up a paper plate and put a bagel and a piece of smoked whitefish on it. "Remember," he asked Mary, "I said I had a feeling I was being watched?"

"I remember you thought it was probably your meds," Mary said.

"Turns out I was wrong. About the meds. I thought it was the police, but boy, was I wrong about that, too. It was a couple of detectives from our health insurance company. Checking out whether we were a legitimate business. They decided we're not. Pretty much accused me of defrauding them."

"Well, I wasn't going to say anything, but it struck me you were going to get busted sooner or later," Nick said. "You ask me, you're lucky it didn't happen when you needed an operation or something."

"Oh, but it gets better," Stanley said to Nick, squashing the whitefish between the bagel halves. He bit off a chunk. "You remember the day we learned about Pete, you mentioned Ronnie Dumat?"

"Sure. Stanley's old college girlfriend," Nick explained to Mary.

"I know," Mary said. "He told me about her."

"He did? Really?" Nick said, sounding surprised.

"She called me a couple of days ago," Stanley said.

"And you're just now getting around to telling me?"

"She wanted to hire me and Dave. As detectives."

"You got to be shitting me," Nick said, spreading cream cheese on an onion bagel. "Wait a minute. How'd she even know that's what you and Dave were doing?"

"Pete. Turns out he and Ronnie were having a relationship. Behind my back."

"Whoa!" Nick interrupted. "Pete and Ronnie? I find that hard to believe."

"Would you let me finish?" Stanley snapped. He took another bite of his sandwich. Chewing angrily, he said, "A couple of years ago the company bought a website called Homebase. Did I ever tell you about it?"

"You might have," Nick said. "Or maybe Pete did. It sounds familiar."

"The jewel in Jamos Company's bankrupt crown. We were counting on it to sell for millions at the auction."

"What does this have to do with Ronnie?" Nick asked.

"Everything. Turns out Ronnie's some kind of broker. Pete convinced her to put together a group to buy Homebase at the auction. Which she did. Only they wanted some concrete data about it before they committed. So he was putting that together. But he got killed before he delivered it. She hired me to find it."

"Don't take this the wrong way," Nick said, "but why you? Why not a real detective?"

"I asked the same question," Mary said.

"It's complicated."

"So she really hired you?" Nick asked. "Like for actual money?"

"Yeah," Stanley grumbled, "you could say that."

"And did you find what she was looking for?"

"Not only did I not find it, but in the process I discovered that Pete was the only person running the website and nobody knows where any of the business records are."

Nick stacked lox on his bagel. He held it up to his mouth. Before taking a bite he said, "That can't be good."

"It's a nightmare," Stanley said. "If we don't find them soon, Homebase could go down the drain."

"When did you learn about this?" Cindy asked, her voice trembling from anxiety.

"Yesterday."

Mary put her hand solicitously on Stanley's arm. "Honey," she said.

"And as if that weren't enough, this afternoon my bank called to tell me Ronnie stopped payment on her retainer check. She came here to get Pete's notes on Homebase and attend his funeral, left without doing either, and stiffed me in the process. It's obvious I'm missing something, but for the life of me I can't figure out what. So that was my day," Stanley said, hoisting his beer stein at Nick in a mock toast. "How was yours?"

Dave draped lox over his bagel, looked around and asked, "Where's Pete?"

★ ★ ★ ★ ★

Friday

★ ★ ★ ★ ★

CHAPTER 22

Consciousness and dread punched through Stanley's alcohol-induced sleep without resistance.

In the nightmare that woke him, Homebase was broken. Its parts lay scattered on a workbench—circuit boards, hard drives, springs and gears. Stanley could make no sense of how the pieces fitted together. The distraught investors huddled about Ronnie. She was assuring them that Stanley had it under control. Stanley knew she was lying to them. He was feeling hysterical. He urgently needed to tell the investors they'd picked the wrong man to run Homebase. But they ignored him. Their eyes were on Ronnie, who was naked from the waist up.

He looked at the clock by his bed. Just after two.

He felt sunk, lost, without hope, certain of impending calamity.

His chest cramped.

Stanley was no stranger to panic attacks, and well aware of their four realities. He forced himself to recite them mentally. The chest pains and shortness of breath did not mean he was having a heart attack. As bad as it was, it wouldn't get worse. With time it would pass. And whatever reason or event seemed the cause was an illusion, an invention of his mind.

He was not persuaded by the fourth, not this time, at least. Panic as a reaction to the conundrum about Ronnie and the missing Homebase files seemed more than legitimate.

He swung his legs over the side of the bed, moving stealthily not to awaken Mary. She stirred, rolled over, flopped her arm across his pillow, muttered something he couldn't understand, but continued to sleep.

Stanley closed the bedroom door softly and headed for the kitchen. He filled a glass with bourbon, retreated to the living room, sat on the couch, closed his eyes and began to drink, his mind making futile, sputtering efforts to achieve calm.

Ronnie's unexplained disappearance baffled him.

Why had she stopped payment on the retainer? True, he hadn't found Pete's notes, but he was sure he had never guaranteed he would. If she believed they'd had a different arrangement, she should have said something.

Or maybe it had nothing to do with his results and was simply out of revenge, to punish him for walking out on her.

Or maybe she never intended to pay him. The implications of that were too dreadful to ponder.

What was she telling her investors now? Was he still a candidate to run Homebase? He doubted it. He realized she'd never given him her address or phone number, and he had no idea how to get in touch with her. In retrospect, that didn't seem accidental.

His mind was drawn back to the dream. To the puzzle. To Homebase.

Stanley had logged onto Homebase a few times but had never navigated the site, having no interest in it beyond its value as a Jamos Company asset. Now he felt an urgency to explore it, to read the advertisements, watch the pop-ups in action, eavesdrop in the chat rooms.

With trepidation, he turned on his laptop and went on the Internet.

The graphics were as he remembered them. The animations were working. Homebase was fine.

He clicked the NEW USER? REGISTER! link and typed in

the requested information: name, home address, email address. He was then prompted to select a user name and password. But one or both of the user name and password he typed was already taken. He was prompted to try again. He entered others, using alphanumeric variations on the first.

Half an hour later he shut down the computer and returned it to his desk, next to a photograph of four young men in graduation gowns, mounted in a wood frame with FRIENDS burned into the top and WISCONSIN DELLS burned into the bottom.

He turned on the television and drank another glass of bourbon.

At some point during a movie about vampires he fell asleep.

Later another nightmare woke him. The clock on the video recorder read five. The unfinished glass he had been holding when he dozed off was on the floor, which explained why the carpet reeked. He fell back asleep.

When he woke again, the clock read ten minutes to seven.

He got up and looked in the bedroom. Mary was still sleeping.

Quietly he showered, brushed his teeth and dressed.

Before he left, he gave Mary a soft kiss on the forehead and whispered, "Thank you." She slept through all of it. She wasn't a late riser, but then she'd stayed up with him last night way past her regular bedtime, consoling him.

CHAPTER 23

Cindy was still in pajamas, white with springer spaniel puppies, looking completely adorable. Her hair was uncombed and her eyelids were smudged from the previous day's mascara.

"I should have called first," Stanley apologized. "Instead of just showing up."

"Don't worry about it." She took Stanley's overcoat and hung it on the hall tree. "Come into the kitchen. I'll make some coffee. Regular or decaf?"

"Decaf," Stanley said, following her. "Is Dave up?"

"I'm pretty sure." Cindy opened the refrigerator and removed a bag.

Stanley studied her as she scooped beans into the coffee grinder. Even at such a mundane task she moved with feline grace. He thought, *Dave's a lucky man.*

"You figure out what to do about our insurance?" Cindy asked when the shrill noise of the coffee grinder stopped.

"Our agent hasn't called back. But something will work out."

"You really think so?" Cindy measured the ground beans into the coffee maker, poured in twelve cups of water and flipped the switch. "Because right about now, I'm pretty desperate." She picked up a stack of letters next to the toaster. "You know what these are? Unpaid bills." She leafed through them. "Electricity. Second notice. Gas. Second notice. Credit card. Boy, do they love me. I pay the monthly minimum and a zillion percent interest on the balance, which right about now looks like the national debt." She tossed them back on the counter. "I used to figure we'd tough it out until the auction, based on your estimate of what we'd get. But I guess that was pretty naive of me. Wasn't it?"

Stanley stared down at the tiled floor. "I have to believe it'll be okay."

"Come on, Stanley. Can't you feel it? The earth rumbling? The sky falling?" Her eyes glistened with tears.

"Cindy," Stanley said. He walked over and hugged her.

She let herself melt into his arms, sobbing softly. Then she pushed herself away and brushed hair off her face. "At least the house is paid for."

"Sell it," Stanley suggested. "Buy something smaller."

"Wouldn't I love to. If Dave's neurologist didn't think he's too precarious to make any major changes, I'd sell it in a heartbeat. I feel like a prisoner here."

"Dave's lucky to have you. He owes me for that."

"Owes you?"

"For pointing you out when I saw you at the Old Town art festival." The mental image of her from all those years back made Stanley smile. "You were the cutest thing I'd seen in ages. I was going to make a play for you myself, but he got there first."

"Really?"

"Really. I went to get a beer or something and when I got back he was gone. And so were you."

"The part about making a play for me, Stanley. Did you mean that?"

"I sure did."

"Stanley. Come over here." Cindy sat at the glass breakfast alcove table. Stanley sat across from her. She looked at him closely and asked, "Why didn't you give me a sign? Any indication at all?"

Stanley stared at her, dumbfounded.

The coffee maker sputtered and stopped dripping. Cindy got up, pulled two mugs from a cabinet, filled them and asked, "Cream or sugar?"

"No thanks."

Cindy carried the coffees back to the table. "I mean it, Stanley. Why didn't you say something?"

"Probably just as well, Cindy. I wasn't very good at relationships back then."

"I had my ways of dealing with that." Her matter-of-fact tone left Stanley with the impression of a woman in command of a powerful and multifaceted sexuality.

"And what would I have done, anyway? Dave was my best friend. He loved you."

Cindy looked quizzically at Stanley. "He told you he loved me?"

"What are you saying, Cindy? Didn't he?"

Cindy wrapped her fingers around the steaming mug. "He never talked to you about our relationship? That we broke up? That we only got married because I got pregnant with Scott?"

"Cindy, are you serious?"

"You don't know that we've been leading separate lives all these years?"

"Cindy, I don't know what to say."

She put her hand on his. "He never loved me. And I never loved him."

"Then why are you still together?"

"We should have separated after Scott grew up. But at that point we figured, why bother? I mean, Dave does his thing, or did, anyway, and I do mine. The only difference it would have made was, we would have had to fork over a ton of money to some divorce lawyers." A tear trickled down her cheek. "And then he got sick. And suddenly it became a matter of right and wrong." She disengaged her hand from Stanley's to get a napkin to wipe away the tears. "Look. I realize this isn't what you came to hear. Maybe you should go talk to Dave."

On the way up the stairs Stanley replayed what she'd said. *I never loved him.*

It made him feel happy. Guilty, but happy.

The door was open. Dave was inside, sitting on the edge of a single bed, barefoot, wearing a bathrobe over a white t-shirt, staring out the window at the back yard. The bed was where the desk had been the last time Stanley had been to the house. A long time ago, Stanley realized. The desk had been pushed to the far wall. It used to be piled with letters, magazines, books, evidence of a busy life. Now it was bare save for two photographs, one of Scott, the other of four young men in graduation gowns in a wood frame with FRIENDS burned into the top and WISCONSIN DELLS burned into the bottom.

Stanley rapped lightly on the doorframe and called, "Dave?"

Dave turned to look and grinned. His robe gaped wider with the movement. He wasn't wearing underpants.

"How you doing?" Stanley asked.

"Okay."

"Mind if I come in?"

Dave started to stand. The bathrobe began to slip off his shoulders.

Stanley hurriedly said, "Stay there." Forcing his gaze above the level of Dave's waist, he sat on the bed and pulled Dave's robe closed. Then he draped his right arm around Dave's shoulder. "Dave?"

"Stanley?"

"I need your memory, Dave."

"What do you need me to remember, Stanley?"

"I wish I knew." He reached into his jacket pocket and pulled out Ronnie's picture and handed it to Dave.

"Ronnie Dumat," Dave said.

Here it goes. "Did you sleep with her?"

Dave's head bobbed up and down. "She was the best."

I have to know. Stanley took a deep breath to brace himself for the answer. "When? While she was my girlfriend?"

Dave shook his head. "Before."

Stanley exhaled, relieved. *Thank God for that.*

"A week before."

"A week?" Stanley asked, surprised.

"At the pledge party. When we brought all those girls to the frat house so the pledges could lose their virginity. Only you were back in Chicago for something. You missed it."

"I don't get it," Stanley said. "What does that have to do with you and Ronnie?"

"She was one of the girls."

"One of . . . ? A prostitute?"

Dave nodded.

"But she was my girlfriend. Dave, that makes no sense."

"I got her for you as a present. Since you missed the party."

"A present?"

"I paid her to pretend she was a student and ask you out and spend a night with you."

"That can't be, Dave," Stanley protested. "She loved me."

Dave shook his head. "No. You loved her. I paid her to keep it going."

"You paid her to pretend to be my girlfriend?"

"That part was Pete's idea." Dave's smile vanished. "Did something bad happen to Pete?"

"Yeah, Dave. He was murdered."

Dave thought about this. "Then he can't use his insurance. Can he, Stanley?"

"Dave, what is this insurance you keep talking about?"

"When he didn't want people to talk. So they'd keep quiet."

"That was insurance?"

Dave nodded.

Stanley said, "Do you mean blackmail, Dave?"

"He called it insurance."

"To keep people from talking?"

Dave nodded.

"About what?"

Dave looked confused. "I don't remember."

Why didn't I think to bring pictures? Stanley thought. Then his gaze fell on the desk. "Just a second," he said. He got up, went to the desk and picked up the photograph of four young men in graduation gowns in a wood frame with FRIENDS burned into the top and WISCONSIN DELLS burned into the bottom.

"What didn't Pete want people to talk about?" Stanley asked, handing Dave the photograph.

"He had schemes," Dave began. He described one with such lucidity that for a moment Stanley thought the old Dave was back. When Stanley prodded Dave to describe another, Dave began to falter. A minute later his eyes glazed over and he stopped speaking.

Stanley replaced the photograph on the desk and left the room.

CHAPTER 24

The neon Nick's Bar sign sputtered unenthusiastically, as if to say, *Come in, don't come in, I couldn't care less.*

Stanley took a deep breath and entered.

Nick was perched on a stool on the customers' side of the bar, feet propped up on the counter, smoking a cigar and watching the news. He waved to Stanley's reflection in the mirror. The motion caused the cigar's smoke to spell an *S* in the air. "Hey, Stan!" he called. He nodded in the direction of the open jar of moonshine and offered, "Help yourself."

Stanley removed his overcoat, hung it on a peg by the front door and joined Nick at the bar. He filled a shot glass and downed it in one gulp.

Peering at Stanley over the rims of his aviator glasses, Nick asked, "Your day any better than yesterday?"

Stanley laughed mirthlessly. "That's the benefit of Parkinson's," he said, toying with the shot glass. "Sweeps away all sorts of pesky philosophical issues. Like hope and faith. You don't have to worry about what each day will be like. Guaranteed it'll be worse than the day before."

"Honestly, Stan. I wish there was something I could say or do."

"There is," Stanley said.

"Name it."

"Bake me a cake."

Nick ground out his cigar in the ashtray and squinted at

Stanley. "You're joking, right?"

Stanley refilled his shot glass and took a sip of the clear whisky. "That's one more thing I really hate about Parkinson's. Nobody bakes you a cake."

"What the hell are you talking about?"

"You get cancer, a quadruple bypass, a hip replacement, people rally around. They bring over homemade dinners and stick them in your freezer. They bake you cakes. But get Parkinson's and everyone suddenly becomes quiet. Nobody does anything. Maybe they just can't take watching someone deteriorate before their eyes. May I?" he asked as he reached for the box of cigars.

Nick responded by flicking his lighter and extending it toward Stanley. He kept the flame going while Stanley fumbled to unwrap a slender cigar.

Stanley shook off the cellophane wrapper clinging to his fingers, stuck the cigar in his mouth and leaned the tip into the flame. "And nobody bakes you a cake."

"I got it," Nick said. "So what can I do for you?"

"What I said. Bake me a cake." Stanley puffed the cigar to life.

"I thought you were speaking metaphorically."

"Angel food's my favorite." Stanley exhaled a stream of blue smoke. "Sponge cake's not so bad, either."

"Got no oven," Nick said, topping off Stanley's shot glass. "This is the best I can do on short notice."

"Then that'll have to do." Stanley sipped at the whiskey. He puffed on his cigar. He said, "I tell you, Nick. Ronnie really had me going for a while there. Thinking about the old times. Thinking about the what ifs."

"What if what, Stan?"

"Did I tell you she invited me up to her hotel room?"

"No, my friend. You most certainly did not." Nick cleared his throat. "Did you go?"

"I most certainly did."

After a moment's silence, Nick said, "I can't take the suspense."

"She took her clothes off. I took that to be an invitation."

"No kidding."

"That's where the what ifs come in. What if we screwed. What if Mary found out." He scratched his chin. The stubble itched. He hadn't shaved that morning.

"You telling me you declined?"

Stanley nodded slowly.

"Probably for the best, Stan," Nick said. "Some stones are better left unturned."

"That a bit of bartender's wisdom, Nick? Truer words were never spoken." Stanley flicked cigar ashes onto the floor. "She played me, Nick. For a fool."

Nick leaned forward and patted Stanley gently on the shoulder. "Trust me on this one, pal. You've got to let it go. If you don't, it'll eat you alive."

"Not yet," Stanley said. "I need to talk it through. With a friend."

"Well, then," Nick said, aiming the remote control at the television and pressing the OFF button, "talk it through we shall." He swung his body off the stool, scooped up the jar and the two shot glasses and carried them to a booth illuminated by a lamp with rotating beer logos. As Stanley slid in, Nick asked, "So what's on your mind?"

"Did I tell you what Ronnie hired me to do?"

Nick curled his fingers over his chin. "You might have mentioned it yesterday. If so, I forgot. Sorry."

"Find notes Pete made about a website we bought. To persuade her clients to bid on it at the auction."

"Oh, yeah," Nick said. "Home Run."

"Homebase," Stanley corrected. He took the cigar out of his mouth and wiped a fleck of tobacco on his sleeve. "Well, that was a lie. There were no investors. There weren't any notes."

"No kidding?" Nick said as he refilled the two shot glasses and slid one toward Stanley.

Stanley nodded. "No kidding. She was after something else entirely." He rested the cigar on the shot glass. "You know what gets to me? Not that she lied about what she was after. That was bad enough. It's the way she sucker-punched me with my own greed." He shook his head. "Man, did she play me."

"So you said, Stan. How?"

"She kept dangling goodies. More money from the auction. Become CEO of Homebase. Not to mention her body, which, by the way, she's kept in damned great shape. I mean, she played me from every conceivable angle. She was good." He picked up the cigar, downed the whiskey and slapped the shot glass on the table. "You know what's weird about Alzheimer's?"

"Alzheimer's?" Nick asked. "I thought we were talking about Ronnie."

"In due time, as Ronnie liked to say. What's weird about Alzheimer's is that it only wipes out short-term memory. At first, anyway. Leaves long-term memory intact. In fact, better than ever."

"That so?"

"Take Dave. You ask him what he did five minutes ago, he can't tell you. But ask him about something from forty years ago, he can give you chapter and verse like he's right there. You know what he remembers about Pete from college? Get this. He used to blackmail people to keep them from talking."

"Talking about what?"

"About something else Dave remembered. Seems Pete was . . . well, I'm not sure what he was. Dave called him a schemer. For lack of a better word, I'd say he was a con artist."

"Dave told you this?"

Stanley nodded. "This very morning."

"You believed him?"

"Why would he lie?"

"I'm not saying he's lying, Stan. I'm saying . . ." Nick finished the sentence by pointing his index finger at his head and spinning circles. "You know. And anyway, that sure doesn't sound like the Pete I knew."

"Why? What do con artists and blackmailers sound like? Take a look at this." Stanley reached his hand into his jacket pocket. "Damn."

"What's wrong?"

"Parkinson's. The simplest thing, like taking something out of a pocket. . . . It's as if the pocket wraps itself around my fingers and won't let go." With an angry shake he yanked his hand out, clutching a piece of paper folded in quarters. He placed the paper on the table and said, "Here you go."

"What is it?"

"Insurance."

Nick unfolded the paper, glanced at it and looked quizzically at Stanley. "Insurance?"

"Blackmail, Nick. Something he kept as a threat to prevent people from talking. But according to Dave, Pete never called it that. He called it 'insurance.' " Stanley shrugged. "Maybe he thought that sounded more polite."

Nick removed his aviator glasses, pulled a pair of reading glasses from his shirt pocket and put them on. He read the paper. He looked up at Stanley. "All I see here is *Millionaire Motorist* and a bunch of numbers."

"You remember *Millionaire Motorist?*"

"Wasn't that a contest some oil company ran? Maybe ten years ago?"

Stanley nodded. "One that Jamos Company handled. Now

you see that column of numbers? Those are cash prizes. Totaled at the bottom."

Nick looked back at the paper. "I'll take your word for it, Stan."

"Part of Pete's job was to make sure that all of the *Millionaire Motorist* prizes got delivered to the gas stations. But since Pete designed the distribution system, he knew the loopholes. You see what I'm getting at?"

"No."

"This was one of Pete's schemes. He rigged the system so he could make prizes that weren't distributed look like they had been. That way he could hold some back for himself. Of course, he would have been smart enough to avoid the grand prizes and just keep the ones small enough to fly under the radar and big enough to add up to some decent change. You get it now?"

"He was pocketing the prizes?" Nick whistled. "Let me look at that again." He studied the paper. He removed his reading glasses and looked up at Stanley. "That's over two hundred grand."

"On just that one contest."

Nick raised his shot glass in a mock toast. "Pete, you sly old dog."

Stanley raised his shot glass with less enthusiasm. "You can say that again."

"Where did you find this?"

"Well, that's a funny story. I went to the warehouse the other day looking for Pete's notes. There were two places I searched first, Pete's old rolltop desk and the room where he verified prize submissions. I started with the desk, but it was completely empty. But first I had to break into it, because it was locked. Then I tried the verification room. The door had been left open. That really surprised me, because I can't remember a time that Pete didn't keep that room locked. And all this expensive equipment was just sitting there. I thought about that after leaving Dave this morning. Why would Pete leave a room filled with valuable equipment open, but lock a desk with nothing in it? So I figured, maybe I missed something. So I went back to the warehouse and really went through the rolltop, and guess what I found? A false drawer. And underneath that, he'd stashed a bunch of papers. That's a copy of one of them."

Nick studied the paper again. He frowned. "Wait a minute, though. Didn't you say this was for blackmail?"

"That's what I said."

"But who was he blackmailing? There aren't any names on this."

"His accomplices."

Nick looked perplexed. "What accomplices?"

"Pete couldn't have pulled this off by himself," Stanley said. "He needed other people to make it work."

"How do you figure that?"

Stanley propped his elbows on the table and rested his chin in his hands. "He was disqualified from winning any of the prizes."

"Couldn't he have used an alias?"

"I suppose. But at one prize per person, he would have needed a lot of aliases. No, to do it right he needed someone else. Specifically, someone to drive around the country setting up mailing addresses, renting rooms or post office boxes here and there, opening bank accounts, all under different names. Then submit the prize winners from those names at those addresses. So when Pete approved them and the contest sponsor wrote the checks, they'd get mailed to legit-sounding names and addresses from all over."

"I see what you mean," Nick said.

"And you know who'd be perfect for the job? A traveling salesman, is who. You know the name of Ed Lind's company?"

"No. What?"

"Jefferson and Maxwell Office Supplies. Cute, isn't it?"

"Cute?"

"The first letters spell JAMOS."

Nick cleared his throat. "I agree it's an odd coincidence, but it seems to me that way back when, Eddie's office was at the corner of Jefferson and Maxwell. Plus he never struck me as the partner in crime type."

"Well, I only met the man once, and based on first impressions I'd have to agree with you," Stanley said. "But I'm trying to be open-minded about this. Easy money can be quite an incentive." Stanley picked up the folded paper and held it up. "Anyway, this wasn't an isolated incident. Like I said, there were lots of these in the desk. Pete was doing this for years."

"But even if you're right, I still don't see the blackmail value. I mean, there's nothing on this to implicate Ed. On the other hand . . ." Nick tucked his hands behind his neck, leaned back and gazed up. "Ed didn't necessarily know that, did he? If he knew Pete stashed this 'insurance' somewhere, he had to assume it named names. So when Pete got killed in the robbery, Ed must have figured he better find it before someone else did. Which means that's what Ronnie was really looking for." Nick looked at Stanley expectantly. "Right?"

Stanley shook his head. "Good guess, but wrong. That wasn't what she was after. In fact, I don't think Pete's accomplices even knew this 'insurance' existed. Think about it, Nick." He jabbed his finger at the paper. "If this was what Ronnie sent me to find, what would she have expected me to do when I found it? Certainly not give it to her."

"Then what did she want?"

"Something my attorney had."

"A legal document?" Nick asked. "That doesn't make much sense either."

"No, it doesn't. May I?" Stanley rested his cigar on the edge of the table and helped himself to a whiskey refill.

"Go easy on that if you're driving," Nick cautioned.

"No amount of alcohol's going to get me drunk tonight, Nick," Stanley said. "You know what I did in the middle of the night? Went online. To Homebase."

"I thought we were talking about Ronnie and your attorney."

"In due time, Nick. In due time." Stanley picked up the cigar and clamped it in his teeth. "You know, I never went online to Homebase before. Funny, isn't it? You have any idea how much we paid for it?"

"How would I know that?"

Stanley shrugged. "Who knows? Maybe Pete told you. Anyway, the answer's ten million dollars."

Nick whistled. "That's a lot of money."

"And all because Pete said it was worth it. I never doubted him. You'd think I'd be more cautious, wouldn't you? I mean, for ten million dollars?"

"Can't disagree with you there," Nick said.

"But I trusted Pete. You know why?"

Nick shrugged. "I assume he knew his business."

"Because he was my friend, Nick. Dave's, too. And friends don't lie to their friends. Right?"

Nick raised his shot glass. "Amen to that."

Stanley took a sip of whiskey and licked his lips. "Damn, this stuff is good. Now, where was I? So I logged onto Homebase. And let me tell you, it's impressive. First class graphics. The home page links to chat rooms, new music reviews, places to buy stuff. So I tried to check those out. But you can't get out of the home page unless you log on. Which means if you're not a member, you have to register. Which I never did before. So I clicked on REGISTER. Typed in my name and email address, made up a screen name and a password, the whole works. You ready for the funny part?"

"I'm all ears," Nick said.

"You'll love this. I got an error message. SCREEN NAME OR PASSWORD UNAVAILABLE. So I tried another. But no matter what I tried, same thing. SCREEN NAME OR PASS-WORD UNAVAILABLE. Or else that little hourglass. One of the two. You get it, Nick?"

Nick shrugged. "I'm no Internet expert, Stan."

"Then let me give you a clue. When Ronnie hired me— ostensibly, I mean—to find Pete's notes, she said they'd be with the Homebase files. The business agreements. The sales data and projections. The operational documents. Except when I went to look for the Homebase files, all I found was the purchase contract. In retrospect that was when I should have figured it out, but I was too stupid to see it at the time. You get it now?"

Nick spread his hands. "You've lost me completely."

Stanley grinned. "It's so simple. The reason I couldn't register? The reason there weren't any Homebase files? *There is no Homebase. It doesn't exist.*"

"But you just said . . ."

Stanley waved his hand. "The home page is there. But it doesn't lead anywhere. Just a dummy site."

"But why?"

"I already told you," Stanley said. "What Dave said about Pete. He was a schemer. You see, when Dave and I got sick, we all agreed to sell the company. We figured it was worth upwards of thirty million, which pegged Pete's share at around ten mil-lion. That number sound familiar? But we got bad news. The company was worth only a fraction of what we thought. So Pete figured, after years of ripping off our clients with impunity, why not the company itself? He bought a domain name and designed a fancy home page and told us we were in luck, he'd found the next hot website and it was available for a song. Ten million. Hell, Nick, ten million in the new economy is chump change. So Dave and I went for it, and my attorney went for it, and with our guarantees as collateral the bank went for it. Then he negotiated the sale, only he was negotiating on both ends of the deal, because he was also the seller. It was just a big shell game."

"You can prove this?" Nick asked.

"Maybe not in a court of law, but," Stanley pointed at the paper on the table, "as far as I'm concerned, the proof's right there."

Nick shook his head, dubious. "There's a flaw in your theory, Stan. Homebase is up for sale at the auction, right? If what you say is true, then whoever buys it is going to discover he's been had. And he's going to look for who did it. And that'll lead to Pete. And Pete would have known that."

"You know what, Nick? You're absolutely right." Stanley took a leisurely puff on his cigar and blew a smoke ring up at the rotating lamp. "Pete was too smart to let that happen. For his plan to work, the first thing he had to do was sink Jamos Company. Because if Jamos Company survived, sooner or later I'd find out Homebase was a sham. You know why Jamos Company never made it out of bankruptcy?"

Nick shrugged. "I don't know much about bankruptcy."

"We were sandbagged by rumors. Stories that we'd been stealing from clients. Stories spread by none other than Pete." Stanley laughed. "How ironic is that? Letting our clients know they'd been robbed as the means to rob our company? Talk about *chutzpah*. You have to give the guy credit."

Nick scratched his scalp, looking pensive. "Even if you're right, what does that have to do with the auction?"

"Everything. Once Pete destroyed Jamos Company, he'd destroy Homebase in exactly the same way. I have no doubt that if he hadn't been killed, the rumor mill would have started to churn about Homebase being worthless. Then Pete would have sent a nominee to the auction and picked it up for pennies. After that he would have buried it, ten million dollars richer and nobody the wiser."

"Amazing," Nick said. "And to think none of this would have unraveled if Pete hadn't been murdered."

"That's the truth," Stanley said. He paused for another sip of whiskey. "But not the whole truth. It's also *why* he was murdered."

"Oh, come on," Nick said. "Now you're off the deep end. He walked in on a robbery."

Stanley shook his head. "No he didn't, Nick."

"That's not what those cops said."

"Those cops, if I remember correctly, weren't sure if it was a robbery or made to look like one. Pete didn't walk in on a robbery. Pete walked into a shakedown."

Nick snorted. "The way I remember what the cops said, Pete was shot by some junkies."

Stanley felt himself getting excited. That meant tremors. He crossed his arms and clamped his hands against his biceps. "Let me try to piece it together for you. Pete and his accomplices had a philosophical difference of opinion. Which is to say, Pete looked at the Homebase money as just him getting his fair share out of Jamos Company. The same thing as if the company had sold for the thirty million we assumed it was worth. But from his accomplices' perspective the Homebase money was a scam involving Jamos Company, and they were entitled to their piece of every scam. You see the problem? So they went to his house to negotiate. To force Pete to share the Homebase money three ways. My guess is, one of them had a gun, and it went off accidentally. That's how he got shot."

"I don't get it. Are you saying there was no robbery?"

"Not at all," Stanley said. "After they killed him, they robbed him."

Nick threw his arms up. "Now you've lost me."

"Pete's death was good news and bad news. The good news was, it changed the mathematics from a three-way split to a two-way split. They could go to the bank where Pete had deposited the money, bring Pete's death certificate and some dummied-up papers and tell a story about how the money really wasn't Pete's but belonged to, say, Jefferson and Maxwell Office Supplies. It was certainly worth a try. But the bad news was, they had no idea where Pete deposited the money. What they needed was a bank statement, a letter, anything with the name of the bank where the money was."

Nick shook his head, looking confused. "So did they or didn't they rob him?"

"They did. They weren't going to rummage through Pete's papers with his body growing cold in the next room. They stole all his papers so they'd have the time to go through them thoroughly. And then they trashed the place to make it look like a typical break-in. But . . ." Stanley held up his hand. "No luck. They didn't find it." Stanley took a contented puff on the cigar and knocked off the ash tip. "But they still had another option. Because there was one other person who for sure knew the bank where Pete deposited the money. My attorney."

"How would your attorney know where Pete deposited the check?"

"Nick," Stanley said, "nobody writes checks anymore. Not on a ten-million-dollar deal, anyway. It's all done by wire transfer. And my attorney would have overseen the wire when we closed the Homebase purchase. You get it now?"

Nick nodded. "And Ed Lind couldn't just call your attorney and ask for it."

"Exactly," Stanley said. "But I could." Stanley took another puff on the cigar and ground the stub against the underside of the table. "So their problem was, how do they manipulate me to ask my attorney for the name of the bank where Pete deposited the Homebase money, and when I have the answer, tell it to them? And, as you may have guessed, the solution was Ronnie."

"So what was she?" Nick asked. "One of Pete's accomplices? With Ed?"

Stanley shook his head. "Just someone they hired to do the job of manipulating me." Stanley took a leisurely sip of whiskey. "And she was probably the only person who could have done that, too. Make me jump through those hoops, believe each bullshit story she told me, without ever once stopping to question whether any of it made sense or if there was something else she was really after." Stanley smiled benignly at Nick. "Dave also told me about Ronnie."

"Told you what?"

"That she was one of the girls at our senior-year pledge party. That he hired her to pretend to be my girlfriend."

Nick's face flushed.

"He didn't tell me if you were in on it."

"I was against it from the moment I found out," Nick said angrily. "I think it started out innocently, as a joke. Dave hired Ronnie to pretend to be a co-ed and ask you out and screw you silly. That was all. But you came back the next day head over heels in love. So Dave hired her to do it a second night. And then Pete got involved because he thought it was funny. I told them they were sick. The whole thing spiraled out of control. Frankly, I'm sorry Dave told you."

"You know," Stanley said ruefully, "I really thought she loved me. And we had the greatest sex. And then one day she stopped sleeping with me. I could never understand it. I had no idea what I did wrong. It broke my heart."

"I know, Stan."

"Never in a million years would it have dawned on me that she stopped sleeping with me because Dave stopped paying her to."

"Look, I know there's nothing I can say . . ."

"Sure there is," Stanley said. "You can tell me how much you paid her."

"I didn't chip in a penny, Stan. That was entirely Dave's and Pete's thing. I wanted no part of it."

"Not then," Stanley said. "Now."

Nick carefully put his shot glass on the bar. "What are you talking about?" he asked quietly.

Stanley shrugged. "Come on, Nick. You think I'm that stupid? Fine. Here." He reached into his shirt pocket, extracted a second piece of paper, unfolded it and tossed it on the table. "The same Millionaire Motorist paper I showed you before. Only without the bottom snipped off."

Nick kept his eyes on Stanley's.

Stanley nodded at the paper. "Go on. Take a look. After the prizes are totaled, the take is split in three. One third to Pete. One third to Ed. And one third to Nick. And like I said," Stanley added, "there are lots of papers like this, Nick. Lots and lots and lots. Going back years."

Nick glanced down at the paper. He picked it up and refolded it. He looked up at Stanley. "And there are lots of people named Nick, too, Stan."

"But only one of them would have known I had a Ronnie gene." Stanley stared at his left hand, pressed flat on the table. The thumb twitched. "We've known each other a long time, Nick. I've thought of you as one of my closest friends. And," he looked up and locked his eyes on Nick's, "friends don't lie to each other. Right?"

After a moment Nick nodded slowly. "Right."

"Good." Stanley leaned back and tapped his fingers on the

folded paper. "Pete didn't need two accomplices to ride around the country opening bank accounts and mailing in prizes. Ed could handle that by himself. But hundreds of thousands is too much money to end up in anyone's bank account without a good explanation. Makes the feds suspicious. Money like that needs to be laundered. For that you need a cash business." Stanley looked around the room, then back at Nick. "A bar would work nicely for that, wouldn't you say? So, how is all this set up? How much digging will it take to uncover that you and Pete and Ed each own a third of this place and a third of Jefferson and Maxwell?"

Nick picked up his shot glass and brought it to his lips. He held it there, staring uncertainly at Stanley, not drinking. He set it down and asked, "Do you think I murdered Pete?"

Stanley shrugged. "Murder's a legal term, Nick. Not for me to say. I wasn't there. I'll leave that to the cops."

"Have you told them this . . . theory of yours?"

"I turned everything over to my attorney. She'll tell them."

"Stan, it wasn't . . ."

Stanley held up his hand. "Whatever it is, Nick, don't say it. If it's the truth, it makes me a witness. And if it's a lie—well, friends don't lie. Besides." He shook his head sadly. "The way I see it, any case for murder is ultimately going to hang on Dave's testimony. And I just can't see a jury buying a witness with Alzheimer's. How ironic is that?"

Nick turned his shot glass in small circles. "Can I speak hypothetically?"

"Sure. If that makes it easier."

"Let's say you're right about Pete and Ed and me. Hypothetically speaking."

"Understood."

"I never lied to you about it."

Stanley nodded. "That's true."

"And who got hurt? The prizes were advertising. The sponsors didn't care who won, as long as it looked on the up and up. The appearance was all that mattered. I mean, they were going to spend the prize money anyway."

"You know," Stanley said, "my attorney agrees with you on that."

"Good. Then you don't need to tell them."

"My attorney already has, Nick."

"But why? Aren't they better off not knowing? They're certainly better off if the story doesn't come out."

"But that's their call, isn't it?" Stanley asked, topping off his shot glass. "Besides, if I don't tell them and they find out later, they'll think I was in on the scheme. Pete cost me my company, but damned if I'm going to let him torpedo my reputation." Stanley looked at his watch and started to rise.

"So why you telling me this, Stan?" Nick asked.

"Because as much as I'd like to feel otherwise, I still think of you as my friend. And as a friend, I think I owe it to you to be straight with you. Notwithstanding the fact that you weren't straight with me." Stanley yanked his overcoat off the peg. "Look, I don't know anything about criminal law. Maybe they'll indict you and Ed. Maybe they'll figure they can't make a case. Who knows? But I do know how big corporations think. And you and Ed are going to be a topic in the legal departments of some of the biggest. If you're lucky, they'll agree with you and conclude that they're better off if this never sees the light of day. On the other hand, they can get really vindictive when they think they've been had. And if they decide to come after you and Ed," Stanley said as he struggled to get his arms through the sleeves of his overcoat, "it's going to get ugly. They'll drag you into the hell known as litigation. I imagine their strategy will be to make you and Ed spend every dime you got from them defending yourself, and then some. And if that's what happens, I think I wouldn't have been much of a friend if you didn't hear it from me first." He picked up his shot glass and downed the whiskey and flipped the shot glass to Nick on his way out.

Nick made no effort to catch it. He watched Stanley leave, while the shot glass, ignored, arced to the table, bounced off and shattered on the floor.

On the drive home, Stanley called Dave's number. A groggy Cindy answered, "Do you have any idea what time it is?"

"I'm really sorry, Cindy. I know it's late. How's Dave?"

"Sleeping. Call me in the morning."

"Cindy? When he wakes up tomorrow? Tell him we solved that case we were working on."

"You tell him."

"And tell him it was his brains that figured it out. You'll tell him that?"

"Go to sleep, Stanley."

"And one more thing, Cindy. Dave's my partner. I'll take care of him."

"Good night, Stanley." The line went dead.

CHAPTER 25

It took three rings and several raps on the door until he heard Mary's weary, "I'm coming." Opening the door, she rubbed her eyes and asked, "What time is it?"

"Late," Stanley said. "You going to invite me in?"

She gave him a kiss, then sniffed at his mouth. "How much have you been drinking?"

"A lot."

"You've got a strange look on your face. What's wrong?" She stepped aside to let him pass.

Stanley tossed his overcoat on the table and dropped onto the couch. "Nothing's wrong."

"Then what is it?" She pulled a chair from the table and turned it to face the couch and sat, scrutinizing him.

Stanley rubbed his left forearm. He was starting to feel nervous, ill-at-ease and the tremors were becoming annoying. He looked at Mary, reached across the space between them and held her hand. "I really don't know where to begin."

"Try the beginning?"

"How far back do I go?" Stanley took a deep breath, plunging forward. "Look. I've been a jerk for most of my life. Threw it away, chasing a fantasy that never existed. I haven't been a good person."

"Don't say that, Stanley."

"Trust me, Mary. It's the truth. Not something I'm proud of. But it has to be said. Because if it isn't said, I can't change it.

And I'm serious about changing, Mary. I don't know how many good years I have left."

"Who does?"

"I can't afford to waste time." He beckoned her toward him.

Mary got off the chair and sat beside him on the couch.

Stanley took her hand. "Let's fly to the Bahamas," he said. "Right now."

"Why?"

"To get married."

Mary jerked back and pulled her hand from Stanley's grasp. "Stanley!" she chastised. "You're drunk!"

"I've never been more sober," Stanley insisted. "We can take the next flight out of O'Hare. There's one leaving in a few hours. I checked. Don't even pack. We'll buy new clothes there. And a ring. Find a hotel on the beach. Stay for a week. Or two. Do something completely impulsive."

"Stanley, what's come over you?"

Stanley flopped back on the couch, suddenly exhausted. He shut his eyes. "What's come over me is I want someone to bake me a cake."

"Well, is that all? You want me to bake you one? Seriously?"

"I'm speaking metaphorically, Mary. Where's your passport?"

"Stanley," Mary said, "you're scaring me with this crazy talk."

"You want to hear crazy?" He rubbed his eyes and began the story. The words gushed out fast and slurry but he couldn't stop. He told her about how Pete stole game prizes, the roles Ed and Nick played, the "insurance" Stanley found in Pete's desk, the Homebase sale, his conversation with Nick.

When he finished, Mary said, "What did I tell you about old girlfriends?"

"I know, I know."

"So what's going to happen to the ten million? I mean, your attorney can tell you where it is. Can't you call the bank and explain that it's really your money?"

Stanley couldn't stop a giggle from escaping.

"What?" Mary gave him a penetrating look. "Stanley, what's with you? I've never seen you this way. Are you high?"

"I already told you. I've never been more sober."

"No, you're not. You're high on something." Mary sat back and studied him. "There's something else, isn't there? Something you haven't told me."

Stanley felt a surge of giddy energy. He reached into his jacket pocket and pulled out a paper, which he passed to Mary. "I also found this in Pete's desk," he said. "A statement from a Bahamian bank account."

Mary read it, then looked up at Stanley, wide-eyed. "Well, there's the ten million."

"But here's the best part, Mary. Look what's written on the back."

Mary turned the paper over. "What is this? Some foreign name? A code?"

"It's a password, Mary."

Mary squinted at Stanley. "Are you telling me . . . ?"

Stanley grinned. "I called the bank. That's all they need to withdraw the money. No proof of identity, nothing else. Just the password."

"Well, well," Mary said. She handed the paper back to Stanley. "You better not lose this."

"You kidding? I'm not letting it out of my sight. That's why I want to fly down there tonight."

"But tomorrow's Saturday."

"The bank'll be open, Mary."

"And all you have to do is walk in and give them that password? And"—she snapped her fingers—"ten million dollars? Just like that?"

"Just like that," Stanley said. "So will you come with me to the Bahamas and marry me?"

"Stanley . . ."

"Yes or no?" He added, "Don't let the fact that it's March in Chicago influence your decision."

Mary grabbed Stanley's face and kissed him hard on the lips.

"I'll take that as a yes." Stanley struggled to push himself off the couch. "Come on. We got a plane to catch."

"Not without a toast," Mary said. She went to the kitchen and returned with two glasses of bourbon. "You want cake? Here's to having your cake and eating it too."

"Amen to that," Stanley said. He swallowed his drink quickly. "Let's go."

"Just give me a minute to freshen up," Mary said. She went into the bathroom, turned on the light, and closed the door.

When she returned, Stanley was prone on the floor.

Mary stretched out her leg and prodded Stanley with her toe. He didn't move.

"You drink too much," she said with cold disdain.

She stared at the motionless body for a moment. Then she went into the bedroom. She emerged a few minutes later carrying a packed suitcase. She set the suitcase on the floor at Stanley's feet, took the paper from Stanley's hand, folded it and put it in her purse. She sat at the table and wrote a note. *Stanley,* it read, *see you around. And thanks for the cake.* She set the note on the floor a few feet from his head. Then she called for a cab.

She carried the glass she'd given Stanley to the kitchen and scrubbed it to eliminate any residue of the powder with which she'd laced the bourbon.

She gave Stanley a long last look. Then she picked up her suitcase, switched off the light, exited and locked the door behind her.

Outside, waiting for the taxi, she made a call. She wasn't expecting it to be answered, and it wasn't. She left a message.

"Nick. Darling. Stanley told me all about what you and Pete and Ed were up to. He's going to figure out sooner or later you hired me to keep an eye on him, so I guess I better drop out of sight for a while. Good luck."

The cab pulled up. She put her cell phone in her purse, next to the bank account statement.

"Where to?" the driver asked.

"O'Hare," she said. "International terminal."

★ ★ ★ ★ ★

SATURDAY

★ ★ ★ ★ ★

EPILOGUE

Stanley woke with a pounding headache, worse than any hangover he could recall, and he could recall many.

He was flat on Mary's floor. *Must have passed out,* he thought.

He sat up. The movement made his head throb.

He tried calling Mary, but what came out was a croak, like a lovesick bullfrog. *Must have had a hell of a lot to drink.* He cleared his throat and called her name, the sound a stark contrast to the quiet of the apartment.

It was too quiet.

It was all alone quiet.

Stanley pushed himself off the floor, walked to the window and looked outside. Snow was starting to fall.

When he turned around he saw the note on the floor.

He recognized Mary's flowery cursive.

He stooped, picked up the note and read it. Then he crumpled it into a ball and stuffed it into his pants pocket.

By the time Stanley reached Dave and Cindy's house, the snow was coming down in flakes the size of golf balls. The weather report on the radio predicted three to five inches.

He pulled in the driveway, turned up the heat for a last reinforcing blast, got out and rang the bell.

"Coming," Cindy called from inside. She opened the door, saw Stanley standing on the welcome mat, shivering, wearing nothing over his turtleneck and jacket, and swung the door open wide. "My God, Stanley. Come in," she said. "It's cold out there. Where's your coat?"

"I left it in the car."

Cindy closed the door behind him and brushed the snow off his shoulders. "Dave's upstairs. But I think he's napping."

"I came to see you, Cindy."

Cindy stared at him, curiously at first, then with a smile. "Well, can I get you a glass of wine?" she asked. "Or you like bourbon, don't you?"

"I think," Stanley said, "I'm going to lay off alcohol for a while."

"Then come into the kitchen," Cindy said, leading him out of the foyer. "I just made coffee. Regular okay?"

"Do you have orange juice?"

"Of course." Mary poured a glass for Stanley, coffee for herself, and carried them to the alcove table. "So what did you want to see me about?"

"I thought about you all day yesterday. What you said."

Cindy looked down at her coffee cup. "Was I too forward?" she asked quietly.

Stanley reached across the table and put his hand on hers. She didn't pull back. "What I thought about was opportunities wasted."

Cindy turned her hand over and interlaced her fingers with Stanley's. "It always comes down to timing, doesn't it?"

"How so?"

Cindy looked up at Stanley. "Whatever I think of Dave, I can't just dump him in a nursing home. And what about Mary?"

Stanley stared out the window, at the snow-covered gazebo in the back yard. "Mary left me," he said, speaking the words dryly, without emotion.

"For Nick?" Cindy asked, disengaging her hand from Stanley's.

"Nick?" Stanley repeated, stunned by the question. "Why would you say that?"

Cindy shrugged. "It was pretty obvious at the bar the other night there was something between them," she said matter-of-factly. "It certainly was to me, anyway. The way they looked at each other."

Stanley felt blood drain from his face, as if his head was a toilet Cindy had just flushed. "How could I not have seen it?" Comprehension dawning, Stanley added slowly, "I always had this feeling someone was spying on me."

"You told me. Those insurance investigators."

Stanley shook his head. "Not them. Mary."

"Why would Mary spy on you?"

"So she'd know if I ever figured out Homebase."

"Figured out what?"

"That there was no Homebase."

"Stanley," Cindy said, "what on earth are you talking about?"

Stanley sighed. "I'm getting way ahead of myself. I have a lot to tell you." He rose and went to the sink, rinsed out the glass and returned to the alcove. "It turns out," he said, "Pete was stealing contest prizes. He was doing it for years."

"Stealing?" Cindy asked, incredulous.

"He'd send them to a cousin, who redeemed them. Who in turn passed the money on to Nick to launder it."

"Nick?"

Stanley nodded.

"You know this for a fact?"

"I do."

"How long have you known?"

"I found out yesterday."

Cindy stood and carried her mug to the coffeepot for a refill. "Nick I never knew so well. But Pete . . . I find this hard to believe."

"That's not the worst part, Cindy. Pete embezzled ten million from the company before it went bankrupt."

Cindy reflexively jerked her hands. Coffee sloshed out of her mug and spilled on the floor. "Are you serious?" she exclaimed. Her eyes darted to the paper towel roll, but she made no move to wipe up the spill. She returned to her chair in the alcove. "What did he do?"

"I already told you. There was no Homebase. The website wasn't real. Pete created it, then told Dave and me he found the steal of a lifetime. So the company bought it for ten million dollars. Except he was the seller." Stanley laughed ruefully. "A real steal, all right."

"And Nick was involved in that, too?"

"Just the opposite. As best as I can tell, Pete did Homebase on his own. Then at some point Nick caught wind of it. I don't know when, but based on Mary's involvement I can guess. She moved into my building last November, so it was probably just before that. He must have realized that sooner or later I'd figure it out, and hired her to get close to me. To warn him when I did and what I planned to do about it."

"I'll bet she was good at it, too," Cindy said, rolling her eyes. "Getting close to you, I mean."

"Anyway, once Nick found out about Homebase, he demanded a piece from Pete. Here's what I think happened. Pete declined. Nick and the cousin kept pushing. But with the auction approaching they were running out of time. So they decided to up the ante. They threatened him at gunpoint. Only it didn't work out the way they planned."

"How so?"

"They killed him."

Cindy's eyes widened. "Come on, Stanley! That's crazy!"

"They didn't mean to. My guess is the gun went off accidentally. Anyway, that's why Nick hired Ronnie."

"What do you mean, hired Ronnie? I thought *she* hired *you*."

"Because they didn't know where Pete had deposited the money. They searched Pete's place for a bank statement, anything with the name of the bank, and came up empty-handed. They could only think of one other person who had that information. My lawyer. Who obviously wouldn't talk to them. So they had to figure out a way to get me to ask her for it. Which is where Ronnie came in. Nick hired her because he knew she could manipulate me."

"So she wasn't a broker?"

"Not even close."

"So she invents a story that she's hiring you to find something of Pete's and twists it into needing you to ask your lawyer to tell you the bank where Pete deposited the ten million." Cindy sipped her coffee reflectively. "Right?"

Stanley nodded.

"So let me guess. You asked."

Stanley nodded.

"And got the bank's name."

Stanley nodded.

"And told Ronnie. Who told Nick. So Nick's got the money. No. Wait a minute!" Cindy leaned forward, her eyes sparkling with excitement. "You knew all this when you called last night."

Stanley nodded.

"You wouldn't have sounded so upbeat if Nick had the money."

"Let me finish," Stanley said.

Cindy slumped back. "I knew it was too good to be true."

"Yesterday I found something Pete hid at the warehouse. An account statement from a bank in the Bahamas. Ten million on deposit. On the back he wrote what was obviously a password. So I called the bank. They said the ten million plus interest was all there, and all they needed to release it was the password."

251

Cindy sat up again. "So the money is still there!"

"When I called you last night I was on my way to Mary's."

Cindy deflated. "Oh, Stanley! Don't tell me. You told her the whole story, didn't you?"

Stanley looked down at the table and ran his fingers over minute scratches in the glass.

"And you showed her the paper?"

Stanley nodded.

"And told her about the password?"

"And asked her to fly with me to the Bahamas while I went to get the money."

"So what did she do? Knock you on the head with a rolling pin?"

"Close enough. She said, 'Let's drink a toast.' Next thing I knew, I was waking up this afternoon on her floor."

"And she was gone, and so was the paper."

"You got it," Stanley said, his face grim.

"I don't know what to say." Cindy turned and stared out the window. The snow was swirling, and the sun was a murky orange blot in the clouds, low on the horizon. "She played you for a fool."

"I know."

"Guess they all did. Pete, Nick, Ronnie . . ." Cindy shook her head. "You do know you'll never see Mary again, don't you?"

"Or Ronnie, for that matter."

"For the life of me, Stanley, I can't understand why you trusted Mary with that information."

"That seems to be my lesson for the week," Stanley sighed.

"What?"

"Trust. You know, those investigators from the insurance company told me the same thing. They said the cardinal rule of detective work was, don't trust anyone. They meant, of course, clients. Ronnie, to be specific. But still. You get the point."

"Sage advice, under the circumstances."

"Sage advice," Stanley repeated. "Except I didn't."

"Follow it?"

"Trust her."

"Ronnie?"

"Mary. I don't know why. Maybe it's just that these meds I'm on make me paranoid about everything. Maybe it was thinking about you. But I didn't trust her. In retrospect, I don't think I ever did."

"Then why did you show her . . . ?"

"When I called Pete's bank, I asked how I could wire the money. They said all I had to do was log on to the bank's website, enter the account number and password, and then click TRANSFERS. So I got wiring instructions from our bank. It went through yesterday afternoon."

"But I thought you said . . ."

"I told Mary the money was still there." Stanley reached into his jacket pocket and pulled out an envelope, which he placed on the table and slid toward Cindy. "I guess I wanted to see what she'd do. I guess some part of me must have known."

Cindy opened the envelope. Inside was a single piece of paper. She removed it. A check drawn on the JAMOS & MOSIT, INC., PRIVATE INVESTIGATORS account. On the *To the order of* line Stanley had written CINDY MOSIT in spidery block letters. Below that, on the *dollars* line, he'd written FIVE MILLION.

Cindy looked at Stanley and blinked. Then she shot out of her chair and darted around the table and threw her arms around Stanley and hugged him. "You figure she flew down to the Bahamas last night and went to the bank this morning to make a withdrawal? What I would have given to see the look on her face." She grabbed Stanley's cheeks and turned his head and kissed him hard on the lips. Abruptly she pushed herself away, her face crimson.

"Cindy," Stanley said. Her sweet taste on his lips was cruelly ephemeral.

Cindy took another step back.

"Cindy," Stanley repeated.

"Don't," Cindy said. She grabbed a napkin and blew her nose. "You and me wouldn't be good for Dave. Major change," she added quietly.

"I know," Stanley said weakly.

Cindy walked back to Stanley and stroked his cheek. "There will come a time when it won't matter anymore."

Stanley turned to look out the window. The sun had set, shading the white snow gray. "Time isn't my friend," he said softly.

"It's not Dave's, either." She sat. "If you want to stop babysitting him, I'll understand."

"And that wouldn't be a major change?"

"I can't tell you what to do, Stanley."

"He's still my best friend."

"I'm glad you feel that way. He needs all the friends he can get." Cindy sat on the chair next to Stanley and took his hands in hers. Peering into his eyes, she asked, "So what will you do? Now that you've got five million dollars?"

Stanley shrugged. "I'm thinking of buying a half interest in a diner."

"At least you can move out of that rat hole and stop pretending to be a detective."

"Are you kidding?" Stanley said. "I've grown used to the office. Besides, I kind of like this detective thing."

"Oh, come on, Stanley. You're not serious."

"You know what I figured out? It only takes two things to be a good detective. One's the ability to put the pieces together. And it seems I'm good at puzzles. The other's a healthy dose of paranoia. And while mine may or may not be healthy, I've got all the paranoia my doctor can prescribe. Plus it helps if nobody suspects you're a detective."

"Then I guess you really won't be wanting Dave around," Cindy said.

"To the contrary. That's where Dave's perfect. I mean, who in their right mind would take us for detectives?"

Cindy crossed the kitchen and placed the check on top of the stack of bills. " 'Right mind' says it all."

"Stanley?"

Cindy and Stanley turned at the sound. Dave stood in the door to the kitchen, dressed in a t-shirt and pajama bottoms with a urine stain in the crotch. He shuffled over to the refrigerator, opened it, peered inside and removed a salami. "What are you doing here?"

"Just having a talk," Cindy said. "Waiting for you to come down."

"Baking you a cake," Stanley muttered under his breath.

Dave put the salami on the counter and reached for a knife. "Is it time to go to work?"

"It's Saturday," Cindy said, hurrying to Dave's side, taking the knife from his hands. "And besides, it's nighttime. Here, let me help you with that."

"Okay." Dave backed away from the counter. He turned to Stanley, scratched his crotch and asked, "Did something bad happen to Pete?"

ABOUT THE AUTHOR

Jon Mills practices corporate law in Chicago. He splits his time between Evanston, Illinois and Hilton Head, South Carolina with his wife and their springer spaniels. *The Ronnie Gene* is his first novel.